YOU'VE SEEN THEIR FACES, perfectly tanned all year-round, smiling at you from the society pages and socialite rankings. You might know their names, or you might just know they're part of the charity-circuit crowd, spending all day at Bliss and Barneys to spend all night limo-ing from one gala to the next.

Take a closer look, though. Does that smile look a little too plastered on? Can you spot the pair whose hands keep accidentally-on-purpose brushing each other?

Can you spot the pretender?

Every picture tells a story. But sometimes it's hard to know what story is actually being told.

ANASTASIA HOLLINGS

HARPER TEEN
An Imprint of HarperCollins*Publishers*

HarperTeen is an imprint of HarperCollins Publishers.

Beautiful World
 For information address HarperCollins Children's Books, a division of HarperCollins Publishers, 10 East 53rd Street, New York, NY 10022.
www.harperteen.com

Library of Congress catalog card number: 2008934893
ISBN 978-0-06-143532-4

Typography by Jennifer Heuer
09 10 11 12 13 CG/RRDH 10 9 8 7 6 5 4 3 2 1
❖
First Edition

Truth is beautiful, without doubt; but so are lies.

—Ralph Waldo Emerson

Every Picture Tells a Story

You've seen their faces, perfectly tanned all year-round, smiling at you from the society pages and socialite rankings. You might know their names, or you might just know they're part of the charity-circuit crowd, spending all day at Bliss and Barneys to spend all night limo-ing from one gala to the next.

Some snapshots from their lives prove that they're just like everyone else, only prettier and thinner:

Here are two girls at Shell Beach in St. Bart's, giggling and spotting celebrities. They're about to take a break from a hard day in the sun by putting some time in at the Cartier store.

Oh, look, now they're three! Back in the city and

having a day of mani-pedis, these three look like they share everything from nail polish to their deepest, darkest secrets.

Ah, after a night of excitement the crew, which is five people strong now that the guys have joined them, laugh their way down Fifth Avenue. This night, like so many others, has been the Best Night Ever.

Take a closer look, though. Does that smile look a little too plastered on? Can you spot the pair whose hands keep accidentally-on-purpose brushing each other? Can you spot the pretender?

Every picture tells a story. But sometimes it's hard to know what story is actually being told.

1

Breakfast Is the Most Important Meal of the Day

MONDAY MORNING, ST. BART'S

Amelia Warner was settling in to eat the most delicious eggs Benedict ever. The lobster/truffle hollandaise sauce was so rich and buttery that she couldn't even bring herself to scrape it from her eggs and onto the side of her plate. The sauce was so yummy that she wanted to eat an entire hollandaise Popsicle. Amelia had decided that she would try not to think too much about the fat content of things this week. She was on vacation, after all.

Amelia's brother, Zach (she preferred the more proper Zachary, although no one else called him that), was seated across the table from her, sawing into his stack of banana pancakes. He was hacking at his food as if it were a tree trunk. Highly embarrassing, even though they were the only people eating in the restaurant of the Hotel Saint-Barth Isle de France. The hotel was a five-star establishment, naturally, and arguably the most luxurious one on the island. Amelia made a mental note to give her brother an etiquette lesson once they returned to their room at their much shabbier hotel on a much shabbier part of the island.

A waiter in a tuxedo jacket—they were all wearing tuxedo jackets in this hotel, unlike at Amelia's hotel, where they wore shorts and . . . well, she didn't know what else they wore; she preferred not to look at them (did they even bother to wear shirts? shoes?)—wafted past their table. Amelia met the waiter's eye and raised her empty champagne flute. St. Bart's was great for so many reasons—the fact that you never got carded not the least of them.

"May I please trouble you for another one of these, sir?" Amelia asked.

"*Mais oui,*" the waiter said.

Amelia closed one eye and peered down into her empty champagne flute as if she were gazing into a peephole. There seemed to be a little blue flower—maybe a violet—frozen into the ice cube. Amelia had never seen flowers in ice cubes before, and she had had her fair share of Bellinis.

Fortunately, Amelia had never had to pay for any of these Bellinis herself. She wouldn't pay for her drinks, or her breakfast, this morning, either. Amelia tried not to pay for anything if she could help it. Her plan was to charge this tab to some random room in the Hotel Saint-Barth Isle de France, and then skedaddle out of the place. Twenty-three seemed like a good room number to choose today.

Hope you enjoyed your three twenty-euro Bellinis this morning, room twenty-three! thought Amelia.

Such an easy trick, really. Amelia didn't understand why no one else seemed to do it. Amelia and Zach were old pros at this. They had skipped out on their fair share of bills before.

It helped that they were both good-looking. Being pretty, Amelia had learned, may have been about good luck and good genes, but how you worked it was all about skill. Zach stood six feet tall, and had floppy brown hair, olive-colored skin, and clear blue eyes. Tons of girls had told Amelia that they thought Zach was extremely hot, but she tried not to think about her brother in terms of sex appeal. Plenty of these same girls had also informed Amelia that they thought her brother looked just like a blue-eyed Johnny Depp, and Amelia could sort of see the resemblance, when it benefited her to do so. Mostly, though, he was just Zach to her, her little brother.

Thirteen months separated them—she was seventeen; he was sixteen—although they resembled each other enough to sometimes call themselves twins; there was something cool, something poetic and mysterious about twins, it seemed to Amelia. People were just more interested in twins than they were in normal old boring non-twin siblings.

Amelia leaned back on her low stool and looked around the dining room, which was located outside, underneath a white canvas canopy on a deck overlooking the beach.

The restaurant had a subdued Asian feel, like Matsuri, or Koi, or one of the other cool sushi restaurants in New York. The view was of Flamands Bay. The hotel was beautiful, but not beautiful in an ostentatious way—it was so quietly classy that you would never suspect that a standard double-occupancy room started at seven hundred euros a night. But Amelia had learned, in her time with the rich and the superrich, that the more truly expensive the thing, place, or person, the more quietly classy it was bound to be.

Amelia's time jumping around from boarding school to boarding school, where her father kept getting jobs (nontenured, unfortunately; that was why they had to keep moving), had really made her a snob about hotels, and lots of other things. Three years ago, when Amelia was in boarding school in Geneva (an experience that had tragically lasted only one year), she had overheard another girl—she was a Rothschild, of the actual Rothschild banking dynasty—say something withering about a "tourist-class" hotel. That distinction had really stuck with Amelia, and she had determined never to stay in one again. From then on, Amelia had made a pact with herself that she would stay only at the Four Seasons. Barring the Four Seasons, any Ritz-Carlton would do in a pinch.

The problem, however, was that there was no way they, Amelia's family—her father, her brother, and herself (their mother had left long ago)—could afford the five-star treatment.

Or even the four-star treatment. Three stars, but only maybe, only if they got a really good deal.

And yet here they were, on a beginning-of-summer vacation at their dreadful *tourist-class* hotel.

When Amelia, her father, and Zachary checked into the room the day before, Amelia had sneered at its disgusting mauve polyester drapes and exclaimed, "Ugh, I can't believe we're actually staying in this hellhole!"

Amelia's father, a classics teacher who existed in a rarefied environment of Plutarch and Plato and tons of other dead white guys, and who didn't seem to have much of an appreciation for the finer things in life, wondered (rhetorically) how Amelia had come to develop such lofty tastes.

Yesterday their father had unpacked his books—his *Iliad,* his *Odyssey,* his *History of the Peloponnesian War*—and had sat down in the scratchy mauve chair by the window and dug into some Homer or Thucydides book or other. He had brought Amelia and Zachary to St. Bart's because he had a two-week job tutoring some vacationing baron's kid.

As their father had prepared his private lesson, Amelia and Zachary had changed into their bathing suits and gone down to the beach outside the hotel.

It should have been fun out on the beach yesterday, but it hadn't been fun at all at first, since their side of the beach had really sucked. It didn't have cute little blue-and-white-striped umbrellas already set up, like the beach at the hotel next door had, and it didn't have blue cabanas, like the beach next door, or waiters in white tuxedos scurrying back and forth with ice-cream-colored drinks on silver trays, like, yes, the beach next door.

Amelia and Zach's side of the beach had only flabby middle-aged people lying on depressing little white bath towels, drinking screw-top bottles of Coca-Cola Light (which was what Diet Cokes were called in Europe, and St. Bart's was indeed Europe, sort of). A few of the fatter women were topless, which was just unbelievably gross. Why was it that the older and nastier people always seemed so willing to go nude in public? Amelia supposed she had to applaud their self-confidence, but . . . ick.

Amelia and Zach didn't even last ten minutes on their beach. The sand was hot on their bare feet as they ran past the beach next door over to the Hotel Saint-Barth Isle de France, a few lots down. Amelia told a tuxedoed attendant a bogus room number (twelve), and the attendant helped Amelia and Zach get settled in folding chairs underneath an umbrella. Amelia drank four champagne cocktails (thanks, room twelve). Zach had two beers.

She loved how trusting everybody was here. That kind of openness was a quality Amelia truly treasured in people.

Now, at brunch, the waiter set Amelia's new Bellini down on the table. He asked something in French, but neither Amelia nor her brother had any clue what he was saying. So they just nodded their heads and grinned fiercely until he left.

Amelia could feel footfalls, multiple ones, on the floorboards of the restaurant deck. She and Zach didn't have the restaurant to themselves anymore. Oh well, it had been nice while it had lasted.

Amelia turned to see an extremely attractive family getting situated in the corner banquette two tables over. There was a mother, a father, and a girl about Amelia's age. The mother, who looked exactly like Blythe Danner, was wearing an Oscar de la Renta (Amelia was a genius at identifying designers) sarong of a dusty periwinkle shade. The father was tall and distinguished-looking, and had a shock of thick salt-and-pepper hair. He looked like an actor too—a character actor, someone who was facile with accents, and won all sorts of prestigious awards. The daughter was tall and golden, and wearing oversize Prada sunglasses that made her tiny, perfect face look sort of antlike (but in a good way).

Once the waiter pulled the table back, the mother slid into the white banquette, then the girl, then the father. There was something familiar about them. Amelia was sure she'd seen them before.

"Isn't that," Zach asked, talking with his mouth full of banana pancake, "Courtney Moore?"

Zach upended some more maple syrup from the pewter pourer onto what was left of his pancakes. He had used just about the whole container of syrup.

Amelia slid her Christian Dior sunglasses up on top of her head. She got a better look at them.

Oh my God. It *was* Courtney Moore, the heiress to the Moore Organic Hand Sanitizer fortune. And those were her parents, the actual Moores. Amelia had probably squirted her stank hands (and other stank body parts) with Moore Organic Hand Sanitizer for, like, a decade! How could Amelia have lived without it? (She was very into personal hygiene.) Immediately the Moore motto lodged itself in Amelia's head: "Clean hands, clean world."

It was so unlike Zach to spot a celebrity, or a semi-celebrity, or whatever Courtney was, before Amelia did. Amelia wondered vaguely if she was losing her touch.

"She's really pretty," Zach said in a tone of wonder. His blue eyes were very wide.

Amelia didn't officially know Courtney, of course, but everyone knew who Courtney Moore was. The *Times* Style section had recently done a piece about her—well, it wasn't only about *her*; it was about the next generation of New York socialites. *Vogue*, *Harper's Bazaar*, and Style.com ran pictures of her all the time.

Amelia knew all the important things about Courtney. She knew that Courtney lived in a palatial apartment on Eighty-second Street with Central Park views. She knew that Courtney was practically on the board of the Metropolitan Museum of Art already. She knew that Courtney had gotten a front-row seat next to Anna Wintour at the Marc Jacobs show last fall.

Amelia also knew that Courtney had a Cavalier King Charles spaniel named Peekaboo—in the interview in *Vogue*, Courtney called Peekaboo her "best friend" and said that she didn't trust people who weren't "dog people." Amelia knew Courtney was a junior at Hawthorne Academy, an exclusive all-girls private school on the Upper East Side.

It was kind of embarrassing and horrible, Amelia thought, that her head, her brilliant head, was stuffed with these kinds of useless facts.

Amelia knew all about Hawthorne: her father had long nursed a grudge against the school because he could never even get an *interview* there. They wouldn't even see him for an *interview*. How humiliating was *that*?

Life could just make you very mad sometimes, if you let it.

But when life handed you lemons, as the old saying went, all you could do was make lemonade.

Amelia dipped the tines of her fork into the hollandaise sauce on the plate. She licked her fork delicately, almost flirtatiously. She made eye contact with Courtney's father.

"I'd highly recommend the lobster/truffle eggs Benedict," she said, projecting her voice across the deck. "It's the most delicious thing. I could eat my way out of a *bucket* of it!"

Courtney's father smiled politely, and smoothed out his *Wall Street Journal* in front of him.

"The food here really is extraordinary," Courtney's mother said, addressing Amelia. She went back to reading her menu. "You simply can't go wrong with any dish on the menu. Last night, we had the most divine ahi tuna in a triple-reduction wine sauce."

Talk of food was nice, but Amelia needed to engage with the Moores on a more personal level. Amelia had learned that if you wanted people to like you initially, you had to talk about things that you had in common, rather than about neutral topics like food.

Amelia removed her cell phone from her Mulberry bag. She typed furiously, although the words were gibberish.

Amelia said loudly, dramatically, "Oh, *Zachary*, I miss our little doggy so much! I keep hoping that the sitter will text me and tell us how he is."

Amelia's family didn't have a dog, of course; they moved around too much, from school to school, from state to state, from continent to continent.

And then Amelia said, almost conspiratorially, as if she were letting the Moores in on a big life secret, "I have a little Cavalier King Charles spaniel. His name is Razzmatazz, and he's the absolute love of my life!"

Razzmatazz was a totally spontaneous name choice. It had not been a good one.

"What a *lovely* coincidence," Courtney's mother said. "Our dear Peekaboo is a Cav too!"

"Well," Amelia said, "I don't trust people who aren't *dog people*, you know."

Zachary kicked Amelia's shins underneath the low

table. Amelia kicked Zachary's shins back.

Then Amelia started talking about dog breeds with Courtney's mother.

"You two aren't traveling alone, are you?" Courtney asked, finally joining the conversation.

Mission accomplished.

"Oh no, no," Amelia told her. "Daddy is back in the room, talking to his broker."

This time Zach kicked Amelia's shin so hard that it almost brought tears to her eyes.

"What room are you staying in?" Courtney asked, and then looked stricken by her own question.

"Twenty-three," Amelia said.

"This is our last gasp before adulthood," Zach added quickly, no doubt trying to step on Amelia's reply before they could hear it in its entirety. "It's our last vacation before we start at Brown at the end of August."

Good old Zach. Amelia reached underneath the tablecloth and patted her brother's knee. She had taught him well. Actually, they had no idea what they were doing in September—their father was still interviewing for lecturer jobs at various private schools. Amelia would be a senior and Zach a junior. Whatever they ended up doing, Amelia hoped to God that they got out of their apartment in ghastly Vespasian, New Hampshire.

Courtney's Blythe Danner–lookalike mother said,

"We know so many lovely people at Brown, don't we, Jonathan?" And then she asked Amelia and Zach, "Would you care to join us for breakfast?"

"You two are twins, then?" Courtney's father asked.

"We *are* twins," Amelia said. "And we'd *love* to join you for breakfast."

Amelia and Zachary exchanged glances. Amelia licked the last of her hollandaise sauce from her fork daintily, gingerly, as if it were a weapon. They stood and walked over to the Moores' table, smiling.

2

Coffee, Tea, or Zachary?

MONDAY MORNING, ST. BART'S

Courtney Moore was reluctant to strike up friendships with strangers. Well, to be accurate, she was reluctant to strike up friendships with nonstrangers too. The sad thing (*Courtney* thought it was sad, at least) was that she hadn't started out this way. When she thought back to her childhood, she remembered herself as happy, smiling, outgoing. She was the one who was always organizing slumber parties at her parents' pitiful little one-bedroom walk-up (Courtney had had the living room as her bedroom) and performing skits for her parents and their friends.

In Courtney Moore's later years (she was older now,

sixteen), she was becoming a cautious, self-protective person. Anyone who said that being a rich girl was a hundred percent rainbows and chocolates had probably been either rich for her entire life, or else always poor. Having a trajectory like Courtney's—poor (okay, *poorish*), then rich—was bound to mess with your head, and with your sense of who you were.

So when her mother invited these two kids, a pretty girl wearing a ton of makeup and jewelry, and a *very* cute slacker-type boy, both of whom seemed roughly her own age, to have brunch with them at their table, Courtney's self-defensive shield went up. The shield, which was known to all of Courtney's loved ones and friends, was referred to by her best friend, Piper, as the "*Star Wars* Antiballistic Missile System" (or SWAMS, as her other friend Geoff liked to say), and it really was not to be messed with. (Actually, Courtney preferred to think of herself, when she was in one of her don't-talk-to-me moods, as one of those freaky dinosaurs from *Jurassic Park* with scales around their necks that shot upright when threatened, like Elizabethan collars.)

The guy and the girl sauntered across the wood deck and took their places at the Moores' table, in the two empty seats across from Courtney and her parents, who had claimed the banquette. The girl brought her fork with her to the table, which seemed odd. Surely the servers here would rush to bring her a new fork as soon as they saw one was needed? Courtney pushed the menu away from her and opened her copy of *The Twelve Caesars.* She pretended she was immersed in it.

Before they sat, the girl extended her hand. She said, "Well, it's time we're properly introduced. My name is Amelia."

Businesslike handshakes around the table. Everyone gave their names: Courtney's mother, her father, and then herself. Neither the girl nor the guy gave any sign of recognition. That was a relief. People who didn't know who she was were Courtney's favorite kind of people.

"And *this*," Amelia said, glancing lovingly toward her adorable sibling, "is my dear brother, *Zachary.*"

"Hey," he said. He raised his right hand to his temple, then snapped it back down, as if saluting.

The truth was, the girl didn't really do much for Courtney. (The boy, on the other hand . . . be still her heart. Sort of like a blue-eyed Johnny Depp.) Anyway, this Amelia girl seemed to be coming on too strong, and Courtney always took an immediate dislike to anyone who attempted to butter up her parents.

That was such a foul phrase—buttering someone up. It was what you did before you shoved someone into the oven.

Amelia scooted her chair in and glanced over at Courtney. She held Courtney's gaze for a few seconds longer than seemed normal, almost as if she were staring at her. Courtney always felt self-conscious whenever she sensed that someone was staring at her.

Since Courtney's parents had gotten rich, Courtney had grown somewhat suspicious of people. Probably because her father had warned her that there were people who would like her only for her (or, rather, *her parents'*) money, and Courtney had tried to heed his warning.

Courtney Moore had begun her life in a fifth-floor walk-up in the East Village, when her father was getting an MBA at NYU, and her mother was running their little soap store on St. Marks Place, back when rents were still cheap there. By the time Courtney was ten, a few years after her mother had developed a foamy organic hand sanitizer that was sold at first only in the store and online but was now pretty much everywhere (that the hand sanitizer was featured in an "Oprah's Favorite Things" episode certainly helped with sales and the ensuing everywhereness), they lived in a palace on Eighty-second Street.

Other kids sometimes mistook Courtney's aloofness for snobbishness. She was actually the least snobby person anyone could ever hope to meet. It made Courtney sad that she didn't have any real friends at school, but Hawthorne girls just weren't her type of people. Yeah, yeah, Courtney knew that the admissions at Hawthorne were extremely competitive, and, on paper, all the girls there were impressively bright . . . but she just couldn't find it in herself to be interested in too many of them. With them, it was all "who's-interning-at-*Vogue*" this, and "look at the new Chloé I got for getting an A in American History" that, and "oh my God, Brooke, are you seriously going to eat all of those carbs?"

That was maybe a little bit unfair to say, but the truth was that there was something about those girls that just made Courtney want to zone out. Such fine educations had done nothing to make them any more interesting.

Courtney noticed her mother's icy blue eyes—"eyes like a Siberian husky," as her father had once described them—fixated on Amelia's blouse. Courtney's mother had become a real fashionista lately, much to Courtney's annoyance. Courtney loved clothes too, and had quite a lot of them, but wasn't there much more to life? Her mother had been quite a formidable businesswoman once; when Courtney was little she used to marvel at how her mother could convince unsuspecting—and not wealthy—tourists from Peoria to buy three hundred dollars' worth of handmade olive-oil soaps.

"That's a lovely top. Absolutely *lovely*," Courtney's mother told Amelia.

Courtney had noticed that her mother had begun to speak differently since they'd moved to the Upper East

Side. Now, *lovely*, *clearly*, and *marvelous* were her new favorite words. She'd also begun to pronounce certain words differently; Martha's Vineyard, for instance (where they had a summer home), had become *Maaaaaatha's Vinyaaaaaad*.

Courtney made eye contact with Zach. (Could Courtney think of him as "Zach"? Were they on such intimate terms already?) Oh, *dude*: he was so incredibly cute, and his cuteness embarrassed her.

"You know, you look so familiar to me," her mother was saying to Amelia. "May I ask how you got onto St. Bart's? Perhaps I saw you on our flight."

"Oh," the girl said, fiddling with her long necklace, made of gorgeous chunky beads of lapis. "This is so lame to admit this, and this is no good for my carbon footprint or my karma, but we flew onto the island from Miami on my father's Gulfstream. *God*." Amelia shook her head grandiosely. "I'm so *embarrassed*. It's so massively *wasteful*."

"Oh no, I think it's *fine* that you came in on your Gulfstream, Amelia," Courtney's mother said as she reached across the table and sort of patted Amelia's forearm through her Calypso tunic. It really was a beautiful tunic, now that Courtney got a good look at it, with flowing belled sleeves and delicate lilac embroidery in a serpentine vine pattern across the chest.

Although there was so much more to life than clothes! she reminded herself.

Amelia had resumed her stare-down at Courtney, although she was smiling with her eyes, so the stare-down was nonthreatening. There was something about her, maybe just a little something, that Courtney found intriguing. Did the girl look familiar to her too? Maybe. Both of them looked vaguely familiar to her, but she didn't know how, or from where. She probably would have known them if they went to any private school in New York.

"Jonathan doesn't like to fly in private jets," Courtney's mother said. Her father raised his eyes, then lowered them back to his page of the *Journal.* "So we flew JetBlue."

Courtney's father was cheap in weird ways that didn't seem logical. Courtney couldn't remember if she'd ever met anyone before who'd flown JetBlue.

Oh, God. She was sounding like one of them again. Like a *Hawthorne* girl.

"I totally agree with you, Mr. Moore," Amelia said. "It seems morally suspect to waste so many resources. Always in life, you have to remember that everything you do has consequences for someone else."

None of the girls at Hawthorne would have been able to put that together. All those girls, they thought they were so politically engaged, but none them even knew what *recycling* was. They would just toss their Red Bull cans and their VitaminWater bottles into the bin for recycling *paper*, without batting a DiorShow-mascaraed lash.

"That is so true!" Courtney exclaimed.

Amelia grinned hugely at her, and Courtney grinned back. It was always a good thing when you met a girl who seemed to have something going on in her head.

Amelia eyed Courtney's book. "Have you gotten to the naughty bits about the emperor Caligula?"

Courtney admitted that she hadn't. She was still slogging through Augustus, who was a whole two emperors before Caligula.

"Did you know," asked Amelia, "that Caligula means 'Little Boot' in Latin? So his nickname was 'Bootsie'! Isn't that awesome?"

Courtney brightened. She was starting to like this girl. She seemed nice. And interesting, which was almost even more important. And Courtney wasn't entirely sure about this, but she thought that the guy kept stealing meaningful glances at her too. He was too devastatingly cute. He seriously looked like Johnny Depp. It was a pretty remarkable resemblance.

The waiter approached the table.

"Are we ready for our orders?" he asked in a thick French accent.

"Nothing for me," Zach said, leaning back in his chair and patting his nonexistent belly. "I already ate."

"Nonsense," Courtney's father said in his no-nonsense way. "I insist. On *us*."

"Banana pancakes," Zach said without skipping a beat.

"That's too kind of you," Amelia said. "I'll have the lobster/truffle eggs Benedict, if you please." And then she excused herself to make a call. "I have to check in on Razzmatazz."

And with that, Courtney thought: *I could like these people.*

I could like these people a lot.

3

Sometimes a Cigar Is Just a Cigar

MONDAY EVENING, ST. BART'S

Amelia (Ann to Zach, and to their father) was drying her hair in their crappy hotel room. *The Price Is Right* was on, and Zach was lounging on the bed. It was a really old episode—so old that old Bob Barker was still the host, *and* had black hair. God, everything seemed ancient and decrepit right about now. Zach was in his wet swimming shorts, and drinking a Red Stripe from the bottle, trying not to look at the mold or mildew (what was the diff between the two?) above him on the ceiling tile. There was no way around it: their room was totally disgusting. He hadn't showered yet, but when he did he would make sure that his flip-flops stayed firmly planted on his feet the whole time.

Usually Zach wasn't so concerned about hygiene. But his sister's influence about germs (and everything else) had rubbed off on him. Also, he had spent almost the whole day with the Moores, soaking in the scene at the Hotel Saint-Barth Isle de France. It was pretty sweet there, and the experience had spoiled him somewhat. After their brunch, Courtney's parents invited Amelia and Zach to hang out with them (although they hadn't said "hang out"; they were more proper and appropriate than that) at the pool at their hotel.

The Hotel Saint-Barth Isle de France was so nice that it was probably as clean as an orthodontist's fingers. The place definitely didn't have a speck of dirt or a microbe of bacteria. He was sure that any random toilet in the Hotel St.-Barths was cleaner than the two complimentary water glasses in the room in *this* hotel . . . *what* was its name again? (And those glasses were plastic, and wrapped with a piece of cardboard that had printed on it, in English, SEALED FOR YOUR PROTECTION.)

"Do you like the name Anouk?" his sister shouted, straining to make herself heard above the dryer.

She tilted her head, and her brown hair fell down at an angle. As Zach watched her brush her hair with her genuine English boar's-bristle brush that she was so proud of, he thought about how surprising it was that this shitberg room even came with a hair dryer.

"Anouk?" Zach asked. "What is that? Like the Eskimo name?"

"You're thinking of Nanook, my dear idiot brother, and it's Inuit, not Eskimo. That was very offensive. You are an offensive person."

"Yeah, whatevs," Zach said, turning his gaze back toward the TV, which was so old that it had those ancient turn dials. Had he actually ever seen a rotating dial like that? It was like an artifact from feudal Europe.

"Anouk is a French name . . . well, and Dutch too, and it means Anne. Or something. Anyway, so I was thinking that I like Anouk better than Amelia. It has more *gravitas.* And it's closer to my real name, which I guess is good."

Gravitas, Zach thought. *Riiiiight.*

Zach's sister had recently started going by Amelia, because she thought it sounded, as she said, "chicer" and "more refined" than Ann. ("Ann sounds like a peasant name," she said, in her God's-gift-to-the-world way.) She wasn't eighteen yet, so the name change hadn't been, like, legal. "Amelia" wasn't official, not that such a detail really seemed to bother her all that much. But on her eighteenth birthday she would, she swore, go down to the courthouse and put through the necessary paperwork to reduce that peasanty "Ann" to a thing of the past.

"Wouldn't your new best friend, Courtney Moore, be confused if you changed your name on her, *Ann*?" Zach asked.

Amelia (or Ann, or Anouk, or whatever her name was today) switched off the blow-dryer and gave her long hair a spritz with some foul spray that was apparently available at only seven salons in the world. She flung her hair just so, as if she were in an ad.

"Number one: Don't call me Ann. And number two: Oh, puh-leeze. Like Courtney Moore would even say anything about my name if I changed it to Nebuchadnezzar of Babylon. She's too polite. She's too . . . docile."

Zach took the last swig of his beer. Their dad was coming back soon, after he finished his tutoring session with the baron's slow child, and Zach had to remember to get rid of the beer bottle before the old man's return.

Their dad still called Amelia Ann, by the way.

"Do you think Courtney's hot?" Zach asked.

He was kind of embarrassed to ask the question, really, because he feared that he was revealing something about himself. Usually, whenever someone revealed something about themselves, in confidence, to Amelia, they could count on her to use it against them someday, just when they least expected it.

Zach wasn't sure what to make of Courtney Moore.

She was Nicole Kidman pale, and Nicole Kidman skinny, but he wasn't sure those were necessarily good things to be. Zach was more of an Angelina Jolie type (who wasn't?), but before Angelina became freakishly thin herself. He preferred to think of himself as a *Gia*-era (a painfully stupid movie, but Ann had watched it repeatedly when they were little kids, and it was impossible to avoid) man.

"Yes, Courtney Moore is definitely hot," Amelia said. "Although I'm *much* more beautiful than she is, don't you think?"

"Totally," Zach said in a sour, sarcastic tone, and rolled his eyes. He glanced over at the TV. Not to be mean, but Bob Barker looked as if he were about a hundred thousand years old, even though his hair was dyed.

"Ass," Amelia muttered under her breath.

Zach didn't offer a retort. The night was young, and it was just better to stay on his sister's good side. He had to maintain a positive attitude if they were going to crash this yacht party, which was what Amelia had decided they were going to do. Whose boat was it? P. Diddy's?

Whatevs.

"Why did you make us leave Courtney's hotel so early?" Zach asked. "We could have kept the freebies rolling all night."

Amelia had made up some crap to Courtney about

how they needed to go shopping with their father. It wasn't even a good or creative lie. But, on the upside, at least they'd gotten to spend most of the day in the lap of luxury. God knew they couldn't afford to pay for such treatment themselves.

Zach and Amelia had stayed at the Hotel Saint-Barth Isle de France until about five o'clock, and they had met the Moores at ten thirty, which meant they had been with Courtney for six and a half hours. (Her parents had gone off to a museum at about one o'clock, thus leaving the children to fend for themselves.) The time had gone quickly, though, with Courtney's quietness and her vulnerable prettiness, not to mention the free food and drinks, and the pool boys who kept waiting on them hand and foot.

The best part about the pool scene at the hotel (minus Courtney, who really was the best thing) was that these pool boys kept bringing them free stuff that they didn't even ask for, all these amuse-bouches, as Amelia had so sophisticatedly called them. (Zach was sure she was misusing the term, but who was going to fact-check it?) So about every twenty minutes, they would come around and dole out things like coconut sorbets, and cold, wet eucalyptus-scented towels, and water mists, and these amazing signature cocktails with ginger and pineapple and God knew what kind of alcohol. They were superpotent.

Naturally, Zach and Amelia didn't start ordering cocktails until Courtney's parents were gone. Courtney didn't drink at all, not alcohol anyway. She just kept sipping her sparkling water through a straw, which made Zach feel really lame, old, and corrupt.

Throughout the afternoon Courtney didn't say much, but she did seem to warm up to them in incremental steps. She nodded and smiled a lot whenever Amelia talked (which was all the time), and she blushed and averted her eyes whenever Zach had something to add to Amelia's conversation (for all conversations were Amelia's conversations, commenced and managed by Amelia), or whenever he ordered another caramel vodka.

"*Zachary*," said Amelia now, "you *always* have to keep them wanting more. Don't you know that yet? Have I taught you nothing?"

His sister was standing in front of him with her hands on her hips, wearing a flowy, hippieish sort of kaleidoscopic wrap dress. When she had hung the dress in the "closet" ("closet" with air quotes because it had one, and only one, hanger in it, and there was no door, just a metal rod hung across a little alcove by the front door) when they checked in, Amelia had very proudly announced that it was a "Matthew Williamson garment," although the name meant nothing to Zach. Was he someone they'd gone to boarding school with in Geneva, during that year that she was always talking about, as if that were the only year she'd been alive?

He couldn't bring himself to tell her that she looked nice. She really did, though.

"Yeah, but have you thought that maybe she would *want* to see us? And that she might call the front desk at her hotel and ask to be connected to those nice kids in room twenty-three?"

"Not going to happen," said Amelia. "She's too timid. No way would she call."

Zach shrugged. He hadn't really thought of Courtney as being all that timid, although she had barely said one word all afternoon. He guessed he had to concede the point to his always correct sister: Courtney was really, really shy.

And Courtney was also really, really hot, and wantable.

"Just watch and follow me with the Moores. Today we played hard to get. Tomorrow we can warm up a little bit. Then we'll spend the rest of the week being Courtney's new best friends. You know what we'll be doing by Wednesday?"

Zach shuddered to think. "Dare I ask?"

"Shopping."

"So evil," Zach said, knowing full well that, for Amelia, retail therapy meant never spending her own money.

"No, *not* evil," Amelia said. "Why does Courtney Moore deserve everything she has? What's evil, brother of mine, is *injustice.*"

That was *so* Amelia. She loved to put everything in some kind of strained, self-justifying historical context. The main point was that Wednesday was two days from now. Two days, acting cucumberishly cool.

Amelia had this incredible chip on her shoulder, coupled with an amazing, terrifying ability to get people to do what she wanted them to do. She knew when to turn on the charm, and she knew when to turn it off.

Zach had his own reasons (read: Courtney) for going along this time.

"Please, please, please don't do anything to screw this up," Amelia said.

"I won't," Zach said. "I promise."

"Do you have any idea how much a friendship with Courtney Moore could be *worth*?"

"No clue," Zach said. "A hundred bucks?" He just couldn't resist messing with her sometimes.

Amelia regarded Zach with something approaching distaste.

"Are you *ever* going to get dressed? Do you really think they're going to let us onto the yacht like *that*?"

He still wasn't sure how he felt about crashing a yacht party in Gustavia. What if huge, stacked bouncers with clipboards were waiting at the dock? But wasn't Naomi Campbell supposed to be there? And the Olsens? That could be cool. It was sure to be a true paparazzi-fest, and as much as Zach wouldn't mind being part of that world, he knew he wasn't. He knew he couldn't pass for Johnny Depp, despite a certain often-commented-on resemblance. Anyway, if they gave him a hard time at the door, or porthole, or whatever the entrance to a ship was called, he was *so* out of there. If the bouncers dissed him, they could just go and screw themselves. Amelia could take care of herself. *Enjoy, sister of mine, enjoy.*

Amelia paraded over to the bed.

"I have a present for you," she said.

She dug into her massive purse, which was open on the bed. After the stink she'd made when they checked in, he was surprised she'd deigned to let it touch the disgusting burgundy comforter.

She took something out of the bag. A cigar.

What the hell?

She handed it to him. A Cohiba.

What the double hell?

"This cigar will make you look like a big man tonight," Amelia said. "I was thinking that maybe you could smoke it and pretend that you're a Russian billionaire."

Zach decided against asking Amelia where she got the cigar. He couldn't remember, but he thought that Cohibas were Cuban. He sniffed it. He didn't know what cigars were supposed to smell like, but this one definitely smelled pretty decent.

"Can you practice your Russian accent?" Amelia asked.

His *Russian accent*? Zach couldn't think of anything to say, and he couldn't remember what a Russian accent was supposed to sound like. He tried something that he considered close:

"I vant to suck your blaaaahd."

"Excellent," Amelia said. "That sounds superconvincing."

Wow. His Dracula impression worked? He was better at accents than he thought.

"You sound *just like* Vladimir Putin!" Amelia exclaimed. She went to the horrible streaky mirror at the foot of the bed and lined her eyes with a black eye pencil. Sorry, but she looked like Elvira. "Oh, and make sure you call me Anouk tonight."

Anouk. Right. Got it. Whatever Amelia, or Ann, or Anouk told Zach he had to do, he had no choice but to do exactly that. That was the way it had always been, and surely the way it would always be.

4

Bizarre Love(less) Triangle

TUESDAY, LATE MORNING, ST. BART'S

Courtney's parents had gone off to look at property in Gustavia with a Realtor from Sotheby's. This had been a recent idea of her mother's—yesterday, after they left Courtney (and Amelia and Zach), they went to a museum in town and did some shopping. Her mother came back all giddy and happy, and said that she and Courtney's father had decided that they loved St. Bart's so much that they were going to buy a villa on the island. The Hotel Saint-Barth Isle de France had private beach bungalows for sale, and her mother said that was probably the best option for them, but that they should at least look at a few other places.

They invited her to go house hunting with them, but Courtney decided she'd order room service instead. Her parents often did things alone, just the two of them, and Courtney had learned to be okay with that.

She wanted to kick back and enjoy the room. Although to call it merely a "room" was to do it a disservice. It was basically its own private house—it overlooked the beach, and had two huge bathrooms, two bedrooms, and French doors that opened onto its very own swimming pool.

Before she ordered breakfast—she wanted what Zach had had yesterday, the banana pancakes—she decided to text Piper back in New York. Piper was her best friend, although she went to Choate. She and Courtney didn't get to see each other as often as they wanted—usually their only quality time was spent over the summer and holidays and vacations together. Piper had seemed kind of upset that she hadn't been invited along on this trip to St. Bart's. (Courtney's mother had explained to Piper that she wanted some "bonding" time alone with her "divine husband and daughter.") Piper never said anything about not being included, but she had been withdrawn and reserved the days before the trip; Courtney wanted to make sure Piper wasn't mad at her.

Courtney also wanted to check in on a certain cute guy named Geoff Ellison. Not that Courtney had any reason to "check in on" Geoff, but she was curious . . .

mostly to see if he'd mentioned her to Piper during these past few days. Even though the three of them had been friends for years, she still wondered if Geoff ever thought about her when she wasn't, like, hovering directly in front of him.

Courtney texted Piper, telling her that she was sitting in her room, on the terrace.

Is there shade? Piper wrote.

??? Courtney typed back.

On the balcony.

Yup, Courtney wrote.

The balcony was deliciously shaded, and the black wicker armchair was supercomfortable, and the view of Flamands Bay was almost heartbreakingly beautiful. The water outside was the bluest blue Courtney had ever seen, and in the distance were mounds of rugged mountains.

Why RU in ur room?? U need a tan!!!! was Piper's response. *Go 2 beach!!!!!*

Piper, who went tanning pretty much every day whenever Choate was out and she was back in New York, loved to make cracks about Courtney's paleness. Courtney thought that pale was beautiful, though, thanks. She was sort of proud of the fact that she was the only white girl at Hawthorne who didn't go tanning. She was the whitest white girl at school, and she wore the badge with honor.

It was probably a lame thing to admit, but Courtney

was mortally afraid of the sun. Yesterday at the beach with Amelia and Zach, she had had just about every inch of her body covered with SPF 100 sunscreen. She also wore a huge wide-brimmed hat and one of her mother's sort of tacky, but also sort of fun, Roberto Cavalli sarongs, which her mother had stashed in her bag. Zach had behaved like a real gentleman by rotating the white beach umbrella as the sun shifted throughout the afternoon, making sure Courtney was always in the shade.

Sun = bad, Courtney typed.

Meh, wrote Piper. *UR having fun in st. b's at least???*

Courtney typed that she was having fun. She told Piper about Amelia and Zach, this cool girl and this cool boy she had met yesterday.

Cute? Piper wrote, meaning Zach.

Duh! typed Courtney.

Immediately after she typed that, she felt guilty. It was as though she were betraying Geoff back at home by even looking at another guy. Not that Geoff would care.

Anyway, Courtney was bummed that cool Amelia and cute Zach had had to leave early yesterday evening to go shopping with their father. Last night she'd hoped maybe they'd call her and see if she wanted to go to Le Ti, the restaurant in town Courtney was dying to try, but no dice. She hoped they wanted to see her again. Now she was beginning to be unsure. They had each other; why would they need her?

But she had had the best time yesterday with the two of them! She worried that she must have seemed highly dorky ("dorkelicious" was one of Piper's favorite ways of describing her) to Amelia and Zach, because she didn't drink anything other than sparkling water all afternoon, while Amelia kept ordering Bellinis, and Zach kept ordering caramel vodkas, which the waiter told them were homemade every time Zach ordered one.

It was just so *easy* with Amelia and Zach. She felt comfortable with them, and she was pretty sure they felt comfortable around her too. When they asked questions about Courtney's parents, they wanted to discuss them as *people*, not merely as some rich society twits. At Hawthorne, girls talked about their parents only in the context of how much money they had, or what they had bought them, or who they knew, or what boards of charities they served on. It was all so superficial. But Amelia and Zach weren't like that. Amelia wanted to know their politics, and the names of their favorite books, and when their birthdays were.

When Amelia asked that about her parents' birthdays, Courtney just about fell off of her lounge chair. Courtney used to be a collector of people's birthdays before she got so shy.

Yesterday, when Amelia braided Courtney's hair in

cornrows (Courtney's mother made her wash her hair last night when she saw her daughter's rad island 'do), they talked about their lives back home. Amelia and Zach told her about what it was like to be twins, and how difficult it was that they had to travel so much for their father's job. He was a big shot—owner, maybe? founder?—of some huge tech company. Was it Microsoft? No, that didn't sound right. Maybe it was Oracle?

Courtney felt that, at the end of the afternoon, she was really able to open up to them. She was even able to be honest about where her parents had come from: the East Village. They hadn't started out with a lot of money; they were totally self-made. They weren't descended from anyone who'd sailed on the *Mayflower*, or anyone who'd signed the Declaration of Independence. They were nouveau riche, and Courtney had never been able to use that term with *anyone.* These were the things that separated Courtney from the other girls at Hawthorne: her parents were the richest parents there (which was really saying something), but their money was also the newest.

So the girls at school looked both up to her and down. Feelings that manifested themselves like this: in person everyone sucked up to Courtney, but she knew that behind her back people ripped on her mercilessly.

But Amelia and Zach were *so* not like that. They were trustworthy, and Courtney didn't trust all that many people. (Did she really trust anyone completely, other than her parents?) Yesterday at the beach, not only did she tell big secrets about her parents, but she also told Amelia and Zach about Piper and Geoff.

"You will really like them," Courtney told Amelia, as Amelia was braiding Courtney's hair. Courtney noticed that she'd said, "you *will* really like them," rather than "you *would*." She had used the future tense. It was almost as if Courtney knew, right away, that she would be seeing Amelia and Zach again. She didn't know how she knew this, but she knew she would have a future with these two.

"I can't *wait* to meet them," Amelia said.

So Amelia was planning on having Courtney in her life too in the future.

I'm going to tell Geoff wrote Piper.

Courtney felt the fine blond hairs on her forearms stand on end. Her heart started beating fast.

??? wrote Courtney.

Going to tell G. that you like someone else.

Courtney's inclination had been right. She shouldn't have mentioned Zach to Piper. *Of course* Piper would use the information against her.

But why? It wasn't like Geoff even liked Courtney anyway. Courtney had nursed a doomed, tragic crush on Geoff for the last year, and he was so wrapped up in his own world (and in Piper) that he probably hadn't even noticed.

Actually, scratch that—Courtney didn't have a *crush* on Geoff Ellison. She was *hopelessly in love* with Geoff Ellison. And just Courtney Moore's luck: Geoff Ellison was hopelessly in love with Piper Hansen. (Or was he?) Anyway, even if he did love her, Piper, naturally, didn't love him back. But she *did* love to tease Courtney about him.

It was sad but true: Piper had a really strong hold on Courtney. Piper was capable of upsetting Courtney more than just about anyone else on earth. That was the *real* reason Piper hadn't been invited along on vacation to St. Bart's—Courtney's mother didn't like Piper, and thought that she was a bad influence on her daughter, her sweet only child. The whole line about wanting to "bond" with Courtney and her divine father wasn't entirely accurate.

Parents coming back soon, Courtney texted. *CU later.*

K. Luv ya, wrote Piper, oblivious—or pretending to seem oblivious—to how mean she was, or could be, to Courtney.

There was one thing Piper had been right about this morning: Courtney really did have to get out of the hotel room. What, exactly, was she doing, sequestering herself in her room—which was a really *nice* hotel room; that was true—while the whole *hotel* awaited? The whole island of

St. Bart's awaited her too. She had to get out and "enjoy" herself, as her parents had implored her to do when they left this morning.

She changed into a white Dolce & Gabbana bikini, and a white silk chiffon Temperley caftan that Courtney's mother had bought her at Bergdorf Goodman. The great thing about the laid-back glamour of St. Bart's was that this outfit would serve her well until dinnertime, no matter where the day took her.

She put her copy of *The Twelve Caesars* in her straw bag and, for lighter reading, the June *Lucky* and the July *W*. Maybe she wasn't as smart as she thought she was, or hoped she was, because Courtney could already predict that *Lucky* and *W* would get much heavier use today than any book.

Courtney walked through the lobby en route to the beach. The other women in the hotel were wearing amazingly beautiful patterned tunics. Most of the ladies were much, much tanner than she was. She hoped that Geoff wasn't totally turned off by her paleness. She hoped that Zach wasn't, either. (There was nothing wrong with thinking about *both* of them, she assured herself.)

The sand on the beach was pleasantly warm between her toes, and the sun beating down on her straw hat felt nice too. Courtney was going to try to think about overarchingly nice things, like the sand, and the sun, and the endless line of white canvas umbrellas and black wicker lounge chairs padded with cushions the same blue as the sky, rather than think about things that were sometimes nice, but also sometimes not so nice, like Piper.

Something caught her eye in the distance. Movement: someone was waving. Courtney squinted through her oversize sunglasses.

"Hey, there, new friend!" exclaimed a voice.

It was Amelia. The day had suddenly gotten a lot nicer.

5

Little Shop of Liars

TUESDAY AFTERNOON, ST BART'S

Amelia and Courtney were lounging on chairs on the beach at the Hotel Saint-Barth Isle de France. Amelia had already been in her chair for about an hour, waiting for Courtney; she had had a *feeling* that Courtney would show.

"Where's Zach?" Courtney asked.

Amelia had just spent twenty minutes telling Courtney how beautiful she looked today, and how supernice her parents were, and how much fun she had had with her yesterday, although wasn't it sad that she and Zach had had to leave and go shopping with their father last evening, thereby cutting their time with Courtney short?

And all Courtney could say was, "Where's Zach?"

Had Amelia's fawning been for nothing? Was Courtney interested in Amelia only as a way to get to Zach?

"Ooh," Amelia said. "Do I detect a tiny crush on my little brother?" She rubbed Courtney's Clarins sunscreen onto her kneecaps. Courtney had offered her the sunscreen, and it seemed rude for Amelia to refuse.

"It's hilarious that you call him that," Courtney said, obviously avoiding the question. "It must annoy the hell out of him."

Oh, right. Twins.

"Nah, he loves it—I was born twenty-five minutes before him, and he totally respects my age and wisdom."

Amelia laughed at her own joke and then spotted Courtney's Roman history book peeking out from her straw bag, and made her tone earnest. "We're like Romulus and Remus. The twins, you know. It's a superspecial bond."

Amelia remembered Romulus and Remus from things her father had tried to teach them. They were twins, and raised by wolves, and were the patron saints of Rome.

"God, you know so much about history," said Courtney. Then she gave a lovesick sigh. "Too bad Zach couldn't come today."

Way back when, it had been hard for Amelia to believe that anyone could actually have a crush on Zach (he was *such* a dork, or at least sometimes), but she'd finally started to accept (and expect) it.

Especially now.

If Courtney was hot for Zach, that could only be good for *Amelia.* If Amelia could slip into Courtney's world, then doors, so many doors, would open up for her. Through Courtney, Amelia could get access to avenues of power that she hadn't ever even dreamed about.

"Zach really wanted to see you today, but he had a tee time at the club," said Amelia.

That was a lie, naturally. Zach was still in bed, trying to sleep off his hangover from last night. They had crashed that yacht party in Gustavia, but they hadn't gotten the night they had been planning.

Amelia had thought it was P. Diddy's yacht, but how were you supposed to tell the boats apart? It wasn't like the yachts had addresses on them. Instead she and Zach sort of wandered onto a random yacht that ended up belonging to an Italian billionaire. All the girls there were wearing the teeniest, tiniest Versace miniskirts you'd ever seen in your life—they were so short, they were basically boy shorts. Everyone on the boat was Italian, and Amelia and Zach couldn't understand a word anyone was saying.

Not that not understanding anyone ended up being a big deal, though, because it wasn't like anyone had talked to them. So Amelia and Zach just watched everyone, and drank the ice-cold vodka shots that were being passed around, and ate about a hundred caviar blinis.

The only time anyone expressed any interest in them happened when Zach was trying to smoke his Cohiba—a bald Neapolitan tycoon-mobster-looking guy in a pin-striped suit and a purple tie came up to them and asked where Zach had gotten his cigar. Both Amelia and Zach felt intimidated and clammed up. Zach sort of freaked out, and ended up just giving the scary bald Italian mobster dude his cigar, although the dude hadn't even asked for it.

After that, Zach got superdrunk. Amelia had never had a hangover before, but if she felt like Zach had looked that morning, she'd know she had *way* too much to drink the night before.

The waiter came up to them and asked for their orders.

"What do you want?" Courtney asked Amelia. "My dad said I could charge whatever I wanted to the room."

Well, in that case . . .

"Could you bring the menu, please?" Amelia asked the waiter, peering over her sunglasses. Were they still serving that divine lobster/truffle eggs Benedict?

Then a thought occurred to Amelia.

"Are you interested in going into town?" she asked.

"Sure! I'm up for anything!" Courtney said brightly. "I'm easy."

I bet you are, Amelia thought.

They took a limo into Gustavia. Amelia was very good, and she was very proud of herself, because she didn't even think about buying anything at Hermès, or La Perla, or Ralph Lauren, or Roberto Cavalli, but she wanted *everything* in the Cartier store. Her father, who, at nearly fifty years old, still lived like a grad student (and made about as much money as one), would have been horrified. "Where in my past did I go wrong to create such an unapologetically materialistic daughter?" he had asked her more than once, and not rhetorically.

("Well, your lack of ambition, and your inability to make tenure anywhere, made my mother leave us when I was eight. Maybe *that's* where you went wrong" was the answer. Although she wasn't mean enough to say it. Amelia wasn't *that* much of a wench.)

Anyway, Amelia was revising her thought about wanting *everything* in the store: she wasn't interested in the engagement rings. She had a lot of years to get under her belt before she would need to do some business in the Cartier bridal department . . . although when she *was* ready for it, she would *refuse* to look at anything less than five carats. Five carats or more: she'd already decided. It seemed important to decide early in life what kind of person you were going to be.

As Amelia and Courtney strolled through the store in silence, Amelia realized that Courtney seemed to speak only when spoken to.

Amelia had now decided to revise her thought about wanting everything even further: she wasn't all that enamored with most of the nonbridal jewelry, either; some of it seemed too old-ladyish—too thick, and clunky and conspicuously gold. But there *was* one section in the Cartier store that seemed to be exerting a kind of mystical pull on her.

"We're going over here," Amelia announced.

She grabbed Courtney's pale hand and led her in the direction of the timepieces, which was a much more elegant way of saying watches.

Instinctively Amelia was drawn toward the platinum watches. She also knew she preferred the ones with square or rectangular faces. (What did that say about her? It was true that Amelia had a fairly square face herself, as opposed to Courtney, who had a sweet, long, heart-shaped face.) Amelia wanted the Tank watch, and the Tankissime, and the Santos, and the Panthere. She couldn't decide about the La Doña style—the face was a sort of asymmetrical trapezoid. Was it cool or not?

Not, she decided.

It was kind of scary, actually, that she knew the names of every single Cartier watch style. Why did she know this? Why was her beautiful brain crammed with such useless crap? Amelia didn't even wear a watch, after all. She had *never* worn a watch, not *officially*—she checked the time on her cell phone, like everyone else.

"Would you like to try anything on?" asked the saleswoman, in a light French accent. She was a tan, attractive middle-aged woman with very good fake eyelashes. Amelia had seen good fake lashes before, and she knew that the best ones were always made of mink.

Amelia shot Courtney a look. Courtney smiled shyly and averted her eyes.

"No," Courtney said softly. "I'm fine. I don't need to try anything on." Then she glanced over to Amelia. "But *you* should!"

Amelia bent over the case. She could feel the heat from the case's backlighting radiating onto her cheeks.

"*That* one," said Amelia, without hesitating.

She pointed to a platinum—or was it white gold?—Tank watch. *Platinum, please let it be platinum.*

Hilarious, thought Amelia, that she, a girl with a father who made less than a garbage collector or a cabdriver (not that those weren't admirable jobs to have, in a way), was trying on a Cartier watch, while Courtney, whose family had more money than God Himself, declined. If Amelia had as much money as Courtney, she would probably try on *ten* Cartier watches *at once*! Even the tacky gold diamond-encrusted ones. If Amelia had as much money as Courtney, she would do a lot of things differently, for sure.

The saleswoman crouched down and opened the case. Amelia held out her wrist, and the saleswoman fastened on the watch.

Amelia extended her arm out in front of Courtney, letting her admire the view.

"Oh my God," Courtney exclaimed, "it looks so amazing on you!"

"Doesn't it?" said Amelia. "It's *so me.* A real classic. It's the watch Jackie Onassis wore!"

"Wow!" exclaimed Courtney. "That's so cool!"

Amelia had no idea if Jackie Onassis wore a Cartier Tank watch or not; she had just made that up. It was getting more and more obvious that Courtney was easy to impress, and easy to lie to. Courtney seemed smart enough—she was a girl who read the classics, after all—but she did seem gullible.

Amelia looked at the reflection of her wrist in the angled mirror on the counter, letting the track lights from overhead make the watch glimmer.

The saleswoman said in her sexy French accent, "It is so *you.*"

"What's the price?" Amelia asked sweetly, batting her eyelashes. It was gauche to ask, *How much is it?* or, worse yet, *How much does it cost?*

"I believe two thousand euros," said the saleswoman.

Amelia had a couple of divergent thoughts: the watch was really pretty cheap—definitely one of the cheapest in the store, but even if the watch was cheap, relatively speaking, there was no way Amelia could remotely afford it.

"It totally looks great on you," Courtney said. "It makes you look . . . I don't know . . . *powerful*!"

Powerful. Right. Amelia liked that, because she knew there were only two kinds of people in the world: those who had power, and those who didn't.

It wasn't fair, and it wasn't right, because it wasn't as if the people with the most power were ever the ones who intrinsically deserved it, like Amelia. Amelia intrinsically deserved it.

"So you really think I'm powerful?" Amelia asked.

"I said you *look* powerful." Courtney smiled, but then must have seen from Amelia's expression that that wasn't the answer she wanted, and added, "I told my mom last night that you should be running a business or something. Or a country."

Running a country. Yeah, Amelia thought. *If only life were that fair.*

"I'll take it," Amelia said.

She had an idea—a terrible, brilliant, sinister idea.

"Very good, mademoiselle," said the saleswoman.

"I'd like to wear it," Amelia said, digging into her Mulberry bag (which wasn't a Chloé Paddington bag, but which should have been) for her wallet. (From now on, when someone bought Amelia a present that wasn't good enough for her, she would do the more honest thing, the thing an *honest* and *powerful* person would do, and *exchange* it for what she really wanted.)

Amelia's wallet wasn't going to do her much good, of course. She had about fourteen euros in it, maybe a five-dollar bill, a discount card from an unpleasant drug store called Duane Reade (she had to get rid of that—powerful people didn't have discount cards from Duane Reade), and her father's MasterCard. The MasterCard had a limit of eight hundred dollars, and was only allowed to be used during emergencies, but, as everyone knew, every emergency cost way more than eight hundred dollars.

She felt around in her bag. She shot Courtney a quizzical look, then shot the same look to the saleswoman. She felt around in her bag some more. She touched her wallet, but no one had to know that.

"Oh no," Amelia said. "Where's my wallet?"

"What?" Courtney asked.

"My *wallet*!" Amelia exclaimed, trying her best

approximation of panic. "I can't find *my wallet*!"

The saleswoman flashed Amelia a look that said, *Damn, there goes my commission.*

Courtney put her hand on Amelia's arm (*Don't touch the watch, please,* Amelia thought), and looked at Amelia with her serious blue eyes. It looked as if she were going to start crying.

"*I think I've been pickpocketed!*" Amelia screamed.

The well-heeled tourists populating the Cartier store all turned toward the watch department, their faces masks of disbelief. Shock, said their silent faces, shock and horror. Pickpocketing did *not* happen in St. Bart's.

"It must have happened when we were walking," Courtney said, looking as if *she* had been pickpocketed. "It's all my fault."

Amelia didn't see how Courtney could have possibly believed that Amelia's supposed pickpocketing was her fault. But Amelia did see how Courtney's perception of events would work in her favor.

Back in boarding school in Switzerland, during that heavenly sophomore year that should have lasted forever, Amelia had played the lead roles in every single theatrical production. She played Lady Macbeth, and Ado Annie in *Oklahoma!*, and Eleanor Roosevelt in a one-woman show, and after every show everyone came up to her and told her how brilliant she was, how she was like a little female Laurence Olivier or Kenneth Branagh.

The sad fact, though, was that she'd never really had the opportunity to act again, in a semiprofessional capacity, since her father had gotten himself fired from the Swiss school.

Now seemed like a good opportunity for Amelia to brush up on her acting chops.

She let the waterworks roll. She sobbed. Then she sobbed some more, crying so much that she was literally hiccupping.

"My wallet!" she gasped through her tears.

Courtney, looking flustered, took a step toward Amelia and patted her back, as if she were calming a crying child.

"I *hate* St. Bart's!" Amelia exclaimed as she cried fake tears. She dropped her head onto Courtney Moore's expensive shoulders.

"Oh, *honey*," Courtney cooed. "I'm so sorry."

Courtney twisted around and peered into her woven bag (Bottega Veneta?). She brought out her wallet (definitely Prada, no doubt about that) and slapped a credit card down on the gleaming counter.

"*I'll* take care of this," Courtney said.

It was an American Express Black card. Amelia had seen one of those only once in her life. But she couldn't remember where. Was it the Rothschild heiress chick?

They were the most exclusive, most impossible credit cards in the whole wide world to get. They had no limit.

Amelia felt sorry for herself for a moment. Her father wasn't even big enough to get a Delta SkyMiles American Express card. Oh, God, the torture of being Amelia Warner! It was so unfair.

Amelia deserved this watch. She deserved so much in life, so very much, even if she was the only one who knew it.

She looked at Courtney, and said, as sweet as pie, "Thank you so much."

6

I Left My Heart in St. Bart's

THURSDAY NIGHT, ST. BART'S

The last two days had been so much fun. Ever since Amelia got pickpocketed, she and Courtney had become inseparable. Amelia had been so upset by having her wallet stolen, the experience seemed to have drawn the two of them even closer together. Times of extreme trauma did this to people, Amelia had explained to Courtney, and often you found that people who were held hostage together or who shared a hospital room soon became as close as twins.

When Courtney was with Amelia, the world seemed fuller and more alive . . . whereas with most of the girls at Hawthorne, the world seemed smaller and deader.

Amelia was smart and funny, and she knew all of this

random stuff (for example: Courtney had never known before that Alexander Hamilton, a founding father of the United States, was born on an island in the Caribbean—not St. Bart's, but somewhere called Nevis, which Courtney had never been to, although she had of course heard of it).

Amelia was also good at picking out famous people on the beach—and there were *a lot* of famous people on the beach. Courtney had always been hopeless at spotting celebrities, whether at the beach, in a restaurant, or at a party. Yesterday Amelia pointed out Kate Hudson, Lenny Kravitz, Matt Damon, and someone named Pia Zadora, who Amelia said had been big back in the eighties, years before they were born.

Courtney marveled aloud at how good Amelia was at identifying people.

"The trick in life," Amelia replied, "is to keep your eyes open and notice *everything.*"

Yesterday at Shell Beach, Courtney did notice *everything* about one thing: *Zach.* Maybe that was why she'd missed out on spotting the celebrities. Zach surfed all day. And he was a good surfer. He was long, and lean, and every time he'd emerge from the water, bearing the board over his head, he was as slick as a seal. Whenever he'd plop down next to them on the beach, he would complain about how much his surfing sucked. His complaints just made him seem even more charming. (As if it were possible for him to be any more charming.)

Today Courtney, Amelia, and Zach had gotten lunch at the Eden Rock Hotel, and walked around again in Gustavia. After her awful pickpocketing experience, Amelia was too scared to carry her own handbag, so she made Zach carry it. Because he was such a good guy, he hardly complained. Amelia felt much more powerful and free without her bag, she said.

Now it was Thursday night, and Courtney and her parents were winding down for the evening. When Courtney told them that she'd sort of paid for a Cartier watch for Amelia, her dad didn't react well.

"She's going to reimburse you, right?" asked her father.

"Of course," Courtney said.

Courtney's father pushed his reading glasses to his forehead, making it look as if he had two sets of eyes, and stared at her for a few moments.

"Let's change the subject," he announced. "Hard to believe that we've been here a week already. Time flies when you're having fun, as the wise man said."

"Jon, don't *say* that!" came Courtney's mother's voice from another room.

He gave Courtney a conspiratorial look and shrugged. "What'd I say?" he whispered.

Her mother wafted into the room, wearing a long flowing chiffon coral-colored robe and black slippers with feathers on the vamp.

"Don't remind me we've been here for a *week.* That means we only have *two* more days," she said, and pouted.

Courtney had tried to block the concept out of her mind. She knew—how could she forget? She thought about it every single second of every single day—that their awful flight on awful JetBlue was scheduled for, like, six a.m. on Saturday morning. But they couldn't leave St. Bart's. Leaving St. Bart's meant leaving Amelia and Zach. They would be starting at Brown in the fall, and Courtney had no idea what the rest of their summer plans were or when she would see them again. *If* she saw them again. Any plans post–St. Bart's hadn't been discussed yet.

"Aren't you two ready to get back to the real world?" asked Courtney's father.

"*No!*" replied Courtney and her mother in unison.

Courtney's father removed his BlackBerry from his pants pocket, put his glasses back on his nose, and started typing something.

"We'll come back soon," he said flatly, studying his BlackBerry screen. "Especially if we're going to buy a bungalow here at the hotel."

Her mother sat down next to Courtney's father and primly readjusted her robe and nightgown. Courtney had never seen anyone who dressed for bed as elaborately as her mother. Before they started making money, her mother just wore boxer shorts and T-shirts to bed.

"And you can feel free to invite your new friend Emily and her brother to our future home in St. Bart's *any*time you like," Courtney's mother declared. "I think it's *so wonderful* that you're making friends."

"Thanks, Mom," Courtney said. "But it's *Amelia*. And her brother's name is *Zach*."

"Right, right, of course it is. What did I say?" And then to her husband, she asked, "Don't you think it's *wonderful* that Courtney is making friends, Jon?"

It *was* wonderful that she was making friends, Courtney had to agree. But she wished her mom would stop making such a big deal about it. It wasn't as though Courtney were some freaky recluse who let her hair grow down to her feet and ate only frozen peas.

Courtney's father stopped typing on his BlackBerry, considered his daughter, then his wife, then his daughter again, and cocked a salt-and-pepper eyebrow.

"Do we *have* to go back?" Courtney asked. A slight nasally whine had crept into her voice. She threw herself dramatically onto the big, soft white couch. "Why?"

"*Courtney*," said her father, glancing up from his BlackBerry, "have you forgotten about that thing on Saturday evening?"

Courtney's mother winced. So did Courtney.

"Oh yeahhhh," Courtney said. "*Right*."

They were supposed to go to some charity ball on Saturday night. *That* was why they had to catch a flight at dawn on Saturday. What was the charity again? Starving trees, or clothes for baby seals, or heart disease in the rain forest? Courtney couldn't remember what it was for; she only remembered that she didn't want to go.

"Why don't we blow it off!?!" Courtney suggested hopefully.

"*Courtney,*" her father said sharply, typing very fast on his miniature BlackBerry keyboard, and not bothering to look up from what he was doing, "didn't I 'donate' about three hundred thousand dollars to this charity so you and your mother can go to this party?"

God, was that how much a person had to contribute to get a VIP invite? Now Courtney felt totally guilty. And then add the cost of the gloriously diaphanous seafoam-colored Marchesa dress (had it been ten thousand dollars? fifteen? Her mother had paid for it without mentioning the price) they had bought her especially for the occasion in the evening-wear department of Bergdorf Goodman.

"Part of me *would* like to skip it," Courtney's mother said. She held her hand in front of her and examined her manicure.

This admission surprised Courtney, because her mother had bought an Armani dress for the evening, and back in New York she had tried it on a couple of times for Courtney, telling her daughter how she couldn't wait to wear it, and the Manhattanites for Poor Children ball was *the* event of the summer social season in New York.

Oh, right, *that* was what the charity was. Except they'd renamed it this year and it was something even more ridiculous.

"I can't *believe* what I'm hearing," said Courtney's father, looking genuinely perplexed.

"We'll be blackballed from society if we don't show up," her mother said wearily.

And you care that you would be blackballed from society because why? Courtney thought her mother was too interested in other people's opinions. She didn't used to be this way. She used to sneak up to their creosote-covered rooftop in the East Village and sunbathe topless. But a lot had changed since then.

"And you'd hate to disappoint Piper and Geoff," her father said.

Yes, yes, he was right. Courtney was hoping that they had forgotten that little detail. Now it really would be impossible to skip the event—for the past few years she and her friends always went to every event together. They were the Three Musketeers. Or the Three Stooges. Take your pick.

But Courtney was still semimad at Piper, and Geoff couldn't care less whether she showed up (despite her hopeless crush), so why even bother? She'd found new friends here in St. Bart's. Nicer friends.

"You know what, sweetie?" her mother said. "Your dad's right. Piper and Geoff are counting on us."

Courtney wasn't so sure about that. And her mom didn't even *like* Piper.

For the first time in her life Courtney actually understood the phrase *digging your heels in*. She really did want to run out to the beach outside their terrace and dig her heels so far into the warm white sand that she would be stuck there. Because if she buried herself in the sand, then no one could take her away. She could dig a huge hole, and she could hide inside it.

Besides, what could her parents really do if she didn't want to leave at dawn on Saturday? Would they pick her up and carry her to the airport? Courtney doubted it.

There was no way Courtney was going to leave her friends. You couldn't just make someone leave her heart behind.

7

Parents Just Don't Understand

THURSDAY NIGHT, ST. BART'S

Amelia, Zach, and their father were having dinner at Le Ti St. Barth, a tavern on the top of a hill in Pointe Milou. They'd been in St. Bart's for a little over a week now, and this was the first meal all of them had shared as a family. As a little, sad, weird family.

Her dad had been working most of the time, tutoring the European baron's idiot son about the decline of the Roman Empire, giving his lessons on the baron's hundred-foot yacht. The baron sailed his yacht around during the day, while Amelia's father and the baron's kid were holed up in the wood-paneled library downstairs.

Every single night their father had come back to the hotel seasick.

"Dad?" Amelia asked. She was thinking about something that had been bothering her all day. "What's the difference between a baron and a duke?"

"A baron is a much lesser honorific," her father said, looking up from *The History of the Decline and Fall of the Roman Empire.*

God! Who came to dinner at Le Ti with a million-page, eighteenth-century history tome? It was all so embarrassing. To add insult to injury, he was wearing a threadbare tweed jacket with leather elbow patches. It was in no way seasonally appropriate attire; the tweed jacket appeared to be the only item of clothing he owned, although he also had a bunch of sweaters.

"A baron isn't as high in the hierarchy of nobles," he continued.

"Why do you *care*?" Zach asked Amelia.

"Because I'm a curious, interested person." Amelia thought about sticking her tongue out at Zach, but she decided against that.

Le Ti St. Barths was a cool, trendy restaurant, arguably the hippest place on the island—there were pillows everywhere, and the chandeliers were covered in feathers—and certain social conventions had to be followed. Also, she'd had to practically beg her dad to bring them there, so she was trying to be on her best behavior.

Amelia did a quick check to make sure that the foursome settling into the table next to them didn't contain a celebrity or two. No stars there—none whom she recognized, anyway—so she checked the time on her glorious new Cartier Tank watch. Eight forty-five. Amelia noticed that she had been checking the time about every minute and a half since she got her new watch. It just made her happy to see the time on her luxury timepiece.

Her father was complaining to Zach about how restaurants with so many "beautiful people" in them made him uncomfortable. He hadn't wanted to come at all—he had made them walk here from their hotel (and Le Ti was probably about two miles away) to drive home his point—because it was "a waste of money." That was one of his favorite expressions: a waste of money. Everything was always a waste of money.

Then she noticed he was staring at her wrist. "What is *that*?" he asked.

"It's a watch, Dad."

"Don't be cute, Ann. Where did it come from?"

"It was a gift," Amelia said lightly.

"From *whom*?" her father asked.

"From her new *girlfriend*," replied Zach.

Thanks, Zach. He always knew exactly what to say.

At the far end of the room, a woman who looked a lot

like Vanessa Paradis was nestled glamorously in a cozy red banquette. She was sipping a flute of champagne. Amelia squinted to get a better look: it *was* Vanessa Paradis, looking as beautiful and as graceful as an angel. Amelia made a mental note to always be as beautiful and graceful as Vanessa Paradis.

"What girl? It's too extravagant. You can't kee—" said their father. But the ringing of Amelia's cell phone on the table interrupted him.

On the caller ID screen was a 917 number, and the name Courtney Moore.

Amelia and Courtney had finally traded numbers yesterday. Amelia still hadn't wanted to make herself too available to Courtney, but she was afraid that Courtney would try to track her down in room twenty-three at the Hotel St.-Barths, which, of course, needed to be prevented.

Amelia put her index finger up, as if to say, *One sec*, and grabbed her phone.

"Oh, don't mind us," said Zach, in the most sour, obnoxious tone possible, as he knotted up his swizzle stick.

What was *up* with him tonight?

"Hello?" she said into her cell.

"Oh, Amelia!" cried Courtney.

Amelia immediately knew something was wrong—

Courtney's voice was wobbly and thick with frustration.

"What *is* it, honey?" asked Amelia.

"We're leaving on *Saturday*!"

Damn. Amelia had known this, of course—they'd talked about it that first day they'd met—but she'd been hoping that somehow it wasn't true, that she'd misremembered. She wanted this time to last forever.

"Oh, honey," Amelia said, "that sucks."

"I know," Courtney said. "My parents are making me go to this stupid Upper East for Lower East party."

Really?

The Upper East for Lower East (formerly known as the Manhattanites for Poor Children) gala?

Really?

The only true social event of the otherwise dismal summer party season! To get a ticket for it you had to be, like, Tinsley Mortimer or Tory Burch or one of the other preposterously entitled society twits whom Amelia loathed (and loved, but mostly loathed) beyond all reason.

"I have an idea," Amelia said, forcing her voice to go an octave deeper. "Maybe I can jet back to New York *with you* to the party on Saturday."

Amelia's father, back to studying his *The History of the Decline and Fall of the Roman Empire*, gazed up and flashed Amelia a steely oh-no-you-don't look.

"Really?" Courtney said.

"Totally," Amelia replied.

"How awesome would *that* be?" asked Courtney.

"I know *exactly* what I'm going to wear."

Amelia did know exactly what she wanted to wear too (a very fifteenth-century-inspired silver Alexander McQueen gown designed to look like chain mail), although it wasn't as if she actually *owned* it. She was already letting herself fantasize about a trip to Bergdorf Goodman with Courtney, and Courtney's black AmEx card.

"I have to ask my parents first," Courtney said.

Parents: always getting in the way of the best-laid plans. Amelia's own personal parent was leaning back in his chair with his arms folded tightly across his chest. It didn't take a PhD in psychology to know that he wasn't a happy camper.

"Okay, you ask yours and I'll ask mine," Amelia said. "Call me back."

As she clicked her phone off, her father and brother spoke at the same time.

Zach said, "There's no way you're leaving early."

Her father said, "I'm afraid you can't leave early. Expedia will charge us if you change your flight."

Amelia felt the blood rush to her face. Money again! It was always about money, and their lack of it.

"Well, what if *they* paid for my plane ticket?"

"Absolutely not," her father said. "My job here lasts one more week, and then you can go home. And who *are* these people?"

The waiter approached their table, bearing trays of food. One of the things that Amelia liked most about waiters in finer restaurants was that they always knew when to show up. Because Amelia was the lady at the table, her meal (ahi tuna, cooked rare) was delivered first. *Thanks, garçon.*

"*They* are the Moores. Courtney's father is Jonathan Randall Moore, and he's a very, very big industrialist."

She wasn't quite sure what the word *industrialist* meant, but she liked the sound of it.

"Jonathan. Randall. Moore," her father repeated, enunciating each word slowly.

Amelia picked up her knife and fork, then transferred her fork to her left hand and her knife to her right. Fork: left hand; knife: right. That was the way Europeans ate. Vanessa Paradis, over in her banquette, was eating like that too.

In the reflection of her knife blade, Amelia checked her makeup. One of the bad things about being in a family with two males was that there was no one to inform her of any fatal makeup disasters.

"Is St. Bart's really *that* hideous a place to be for

another week?" asked their father.

Zach dug into his steak au poivre *before* their father had even been served. She had so much work to do on him.

"Yeah, look on the br—" Zach said. He was speaking with his mouth full of food. (So very much work to do.) "Look on the bright side."

Maybe that was pretty sound advice, now as in every other time in life: look on the bright side. Because even if she didn't get to go back to New York on Saturday, she would just have to revise her plan. All truly great people were supremely adaptive, of course. The only thing that mattered was that Courtney Moore didn't forget about her before Amelia got back into her world.

And Amelia would make sure she didn't.

8

It's Not My Party, but I'll Still Cry If I Want To

SUNDAY NIGHT, ST. BART'S

Amelia—Ann, whatever—had been in a real "funk," as their dad said, since Courtney left for New York the morning before. She had barely wanted to leave their hotel, crappy though it was, at all.

Yesterday morning Amelia got a wake-up call (yes, apparently even the crappiest hotels offered wake-up call service) at four thirty. She called a taxi to take her to the airport to see off Courtney and her parents. After the phone rang, their father rolled over in his cot—he was sleeping in the foldout cot in the room, while Amelia and Zach each got their own twin bed—and mumbled,

". . . insists on going to the airport . . . Zachary, go with your sister. . . ."

So Zach, because he was a good brother (sort of) and a good boy (mostly) did go to the airport with his sister.

He had his own ulterior motives.

And his ulterior motive looked pretty hot yesterday at dawn, in the airport, straddling all of her mother's trunks that lay scattered on the floor at the check-in desk.

Amelia made Courtney promise that she would call as soon as she landed, and call during the party that night, and call when she got home from the party. So much for playing hard to get.

Zach felt weird about hugging Courtney good-bye (although he wanted to), and he decided that he would shake her hand instead. But when he was reaching for her hand, Courtney went right in for a great big huge hug. Zach wasn't much of a hugger—no one in his family was anymore—so it felt awkward at first. He could smell Courtney's hair (something kind of citrusy, maybe?) and feel the softness of her T-shirt (it looked like a regular shirt, but Zach was pretty sure none of his T-shirts felt like this). They held the hug for what seemed like a very long time, Zach felt.

As he was shaking Courtney's parents' hands, Courtney said, "I'm so glad I met you guys."

Amelia and Zach had gone back to their hotel room

and napped for a couple of hours. They spent the rest of the day snorkeling and parasailing. Amelia had flirted so aggressively and so shamelessly with the guys at the snorkeling and parasailing booths that the guys didn't charge them for either.

Last night they went back to Le Ti, this time without their father, and this time with a less subdued night in mind. There were belly dancers on tables, and everyone was smoking inside (so unlike New Hampshire, or even New York). Amelia kept ordering rum and Diet Cokes, and checking her phone to see if Courtney had texted her. Amelia's mood got more and more sour as the night progressed, when it became clear that Courtney wasn't going to call or text from New York. Zach might have checked his phone too, but he and Courtney hadn't exchanged numbers. He supposed (hoped) that Courtney figured having Amelia's was as good as having Zach's, and not that she didn't care about ever seeing him again.

Today Amelia and Zach went back to Shell Beach, where they had been a few days before with Courtney. The warm heat of the sun should have made his sister happy, but she just sat on a towel in the sand, flipping forlornly through her *In Style.* Then, suddenly, she flung the magazine violently out into the sand.

Amelia extended her thin, tan arm in front of her, considering her new Cartier (Zach knew the brand because

Amelia wouldn't shut up about it), and said, "You know what, Zach? My new timepiece is not bringing me any joy at all."

Zach didn't really care enough to ask why her watch wasn't bringing her joy—was it because she recognized how essentially sad it was to rely on your personal possessions to bring you happiness, or did looking at the watch make her feel guilty, because Courtney had bought it for her, or maybe the watch reminded her of Courtney, and the idea of Courtney made her sad because she was gone?

It was hard sometimes to know what Amelia meant. Zach's sister was an enigma. She had a tendency to get really moody if she felt that things weren't going her way.

Zach was bummed too that Courtney hadn't called, but he was in St. Bart's, for chrissakes, and was trying to make the most of it.

Amelia had spent the rest of the day on the computer in the lobby. This was very unlike her, since she loved making fun of other girls who spent these most precious hours of their youth perusing Perez Hilton and TMZ, but there Amelia was, camped out in the lobby of their hotel, a big bottle of Fiji water next to her on the ugly lobby desk that she had complained looked as if it had come from the bargain basement of hell. Amelia was watching some video from a morning talk show about an underwearless starlet's nervous breakdown.

"Hey. What are you doing?" Zach asked.

"Nursing my depression," Amelia said. She turned her head to Zach and made much of dramatically raising an eyebrow.

"You're depressed because we're leaving St. Bart's soon?" Zach asked. Sometimes he just liked to push his sister's buttons. It was kind of like a science experiment—you could have a reasoned hypothesis, but you just never knew what kind of result you'd get.

"I can't leave St. Bart's soon enough!" Amelia swiveled a one-eighty on the cheap office chair. "Aren't you *so* sick of it here? I've *had it* with the smells of coconut and pineapple, and wearing a bathing suit all the time, and *beach fatigue.*"

"Yeah," Zach said. "Beach fatigue. Pretty rough stuff."

"Oh, and you know what else sucks about it here? It's June. It's the *off-season*! That means that *no one* who's *anyone* would be *caught dead* in St. Bart's now."

"The Moore family was just here. So it can't be *too* bad to be in St. Bart's in June."

"But that was *last week*! Don't you know *anything* about the tourist calendar?"

Sometimes it drove Zach crazy how influenced his sister was by some retarded social custom, how she felt like what she did mattered in the eyes of, like, *society*. Their mother had been—*was*, although, these days Zach tended to think of her in the past tense—like that too. He particularly remembered how, when they were young, their mother would often voice all sorts of free-floating complaints about how embarrassed she was to tell people that her husband hadn't even made tenure yet. Even when he was a little kid, Zach remembered wondering why his mother felt that she had to tell people anything at all about his job.

Amelia's phone lay by her Fiji bottle. She glared at it. "I can't believe Courtney hasn't called."

"Hey, I have a crazy idea," Zach said. "Why don't *you* call *her*?"

"Can't," Amelia said. "Too desperate."

Zach was very close to asking his sister if every single action she'd ever taken in her life was this calculated. He couldn't remember back to a time when she'd behaved any differently, so maybe she *had* always been this way.

"Don't you think that maybe she *wants* to hear from you?" asked Zach.

"Maybe," Amelia said, "but she probably wants to hear from you even more than she wants to hear from me." She tried to say this lightly, but Zach could tell it annoyed the hell out of her. And even if he wasn't so sure it was true, he liked hearing her say it anyway.

Zach reached for the phone—half jokingly, and half not.

Amelia batted his hand away.

"Don't you *dare*," Amelia said. "I know it's hard, but this is all part of my grand plan. *Trust me.*"

"So then why are you so upset?"

"I *am* human, you know," she replied. "Despite rumors to the contrary."

Zach wheeled out the other chair from underneath the desk. It was kind of weird that the hotel had these upholstered office chairs in the lobby, but, as Amelia had said numerous times during the week, what could you expect from a tourist-class hotel?

Amelia started typing. Zach had a feeling he knew what his sister was up to. . . .

"I wonder if there are pictures from last night?" he asked.

She smiled at him. "Great minds think alike."

She went first to this stupid socialite-ranking website that Zach knew was, unfortunately, Amelia's home page.

Listed today at number five: Courtney Moore.

The page said that her rank had gone up by eighty-three points in the last day. Underneath the ranking was a link to pictures. Amelia clicked on it.

Picture after picture showed a beaming Courtney, looking gorgeous in a pretty dress.

"Doesn't her dress look like it's made out of dragonfly wings?" Amelia asked.

That wasn't exactly what Zach had been thinking. "I guess."

"I'm ill," said Amelia.

Zach concurred. He knew that Courtney had invited both Amelia and him to the party, but still, looking at the pictures made him feel cast out of a world that wanted nothing to do with him. The pictures painfully underscored the differences between Courtney's life and Zach and Amelia's.

Amelia enlarged a thumbnail picture of Courtney flanked by a fair-haired guy and a fair-haired girl. The guy had a prominent jawline, a high forehead, and a hairline that looked like it was going to start receding any minute now—basically, he had that overbred look of the aristocracy. So unlike Zach's own dark looks.

They clicked on another picture—this one was of only Courtney and the guy. In this picture the dude's hand was circling Courtney's waist in a too-intimate way.

Zach felt as if he'd been kicked in the chest.

"Who is *that*?" he asked, trying to hide his resentment.

"That," Amelia replied, "is Geoff. Spelled with a G."

Gag. Geoff with a G was wearing a tux, which made Zach doubly ill. Only douches wore tuxes. (And spelled Geoff with a G.)

"And the girl," Amelia continued, "is Piper Hansen. She's Courtney's best friend. And I *know* that I don't like her."

Zach looked around the shabby lobby, decorated with cheap furniture and populated with tacky tourists with fanny packs and cameras on straps around their necks, and suddenly felt very melancholy.

"Look at them," Zach said, gesturing to the computer screen. "They're the beautiful people."

He knew it was a cheesy sentiment, something his father would've said, but cheesy sentiments were the norm when you were feeling sorry for yourself.

"Ex*cuse* me. We're beautiful people too," Amelia said sharply.

It was funny; it occurred to Zach that he and his sister were like a symbiotic, self-correcting unit—when she was down, he was up; now, when he was down, she was up. When the three of them had been hanging out at Shell Beach earlier in the week, Courtney had made the comment that "you guys"—meaning Zach and Amelia—"really seem to balance each other out so well."

That had been an insightful comment, it seemed now. Almost as if Courtney had understood, in a very brief time, who Zach and Amelia were, and what they were about.

"Do you really think we can compete in their world?" asked Zach.

"Of course we can, dear little brother," Amelia said, then clicked off the stupid party-picture website and planted a discreet kiss on Zach's forehead. "She loves us."

"And what about us?" he asked. "Do we love her?"

It was kind of an obnoxious question to ask, because Amelia hated any kind of line of inquiry that required self-analysis.

Amelia's face turned as red as a rubber ball, and she looked away.

Her phone on the desk vibrated. Amelia and Zach exchanged looks, and both lunged for the phone at the same time.

Amelia got it first, naturally. The caller ID said, COURTNEY MOORE.

She clicked on the call button. "Hello, my dear," Amelia said into the phone, sounding so lax even Zach wouldn't have believed she'd spent the last day waiting for this very call.

Zach felt his heart race. He had a desire to grab the phone from her and ask Courtney about that tuxedo-wearing douche Geoff. Because surely Geoff would turn out to be maybe a cousin, or her semiretarded half brother, or her gay best friend, or someone.

"Oh, right, right, you had that *party* last night," Amelia said. "I'd *totally* forgotten about it. How was it?"

Amelia gave a few assorted "ooohs" and "ahhhs" and "oh my Gods" into the phone, seemingly very impressed and amused by whatever Courtney was telling her about her adventures last night.

"That's *so* nice of you to say," Amelia said. "Well, I wish we could have been there too."

Who was Amelia kidding, that they were entitled to be a part of the beautiful world? Zach imagined himself at the party—in an ill-fitting rented tux with a crooked bow tie, saying the wrong thing to everyone, probably dribbling bean dip down the front of his shirt. You know what? Thank God he *hadn't* been at the party last night, actually. As much as he did want to give that guy Geoff a good beat-down. Geoff with a G.

"Next weekend?" Amelia asked, flexing her wrist, watching how her Cartier "timepiece" reflected the light and scattered it on the lobby walls. "I think we might be busy next weekend, but it sounds so fun to come out to your house in East Hampton. Maybe the following weekend?"

Amelia knew full well that they were free next weekend, and every weekend thereafter, but Zach understood that his sister was still playing hard to get . . . sort of. Zach sat back in his cheap office chair and reminded himself that he had to trust Amelia and go along with whatever she concocted. It was all part of her grand plan.

9

That's What Friends Are For

MONDAY, EARLY AFTERNOON, NEW YORK

Jeffrey was hands-down the best shoe store in New York, which meant that it was just about the greatest shoe store in the entire world. The selection and service were unbeatable, although Courtney's mother didn't understand why her daughter had to go all the way downtown to buy her shoes. "Why don't you just go to Barneys, like everyone else?" she had asked this morning, as Courtney was getting ready to go.

And it was true that Jeffrey, which was located in the Meatpacking District, wasn't the most convenient place to get to from the Upper East Side. In a taxi (Courtney hadn't taken the subway in, like, five years) the trip to

Fourteenth Street and Tenth Avenue could take half an hour, forty minutes in bad traffic.

Although Courtney's mother had lived in the East Village for almost a decade, she preferred to ignore that part of her life. She liked to say that she now considered anything south of, say, Forty-second Street a wasteland, a dark and dangerous netherworld, and she and Courtney's father ventured into the Forties only when they had theater tickets. Courtney knew the real reason her mother didn't like going downtown, though: she'd gotten into a cab accident last year (not a big deal, although she had to wear a sling around her arm for five days) and had developed a fear of taxis.

One of the reasons Courtney liked Jeffrey so much was that she had her own personal shoe salesman there. His name was Alvero, and Courtney was supposed to call him whenever she was planning a trip downtown, so he could pull shoes in her size (seven and a half) that he believed might interest her. Sometimes he even got her a cupcake from Billy's Bakery on Ninth Avenue, which he would put out on a white china plate for her.

Today the plan was to do a little shoe shopping, then meet Piper and Geoff a couple of blocks away at Pastis for brunch. Courtney had forgotten to call Alvero, though, to give him a heads-up that she was coming—she had just sort of assumed that he would be in the shoe salon at

Jeffrey because he was always in the shoe salon at Jeffrey. Courtney had probably been shoe shopping at the store at least twenty times, and Alvero was always there.

No sooner had Courtney run a finger over a rich brown Balenciaga boot with a heavy, complicated buckle than a salesman who wasn't Alvero swooped in and asked her if she wanted to try the boots on.

Courtney replied that she did want to try on the Balenciagas, although where was Alvero? He was her usual salesman, she said.

She felt as if she were betraying him by even talking to someone else in the shoe salon. Courtney was a very loyal person, and she hated the idea of betraying anyone.

"He doesn't work on Mondays, honey," replied the salesclerk matter-of-factly.

As Courtney waited for the non-Alvero salesman to return from the stockroom with her boots, she meandered around the shoe store. It really was such a wider and better selection than the Barneys shoe department. She had to remember to tell her mother later today how Jeffrey's shoe selection blew Barneys away.

Even such a ringing endorsement probably wouldn't be enough to convince her mother to come downtown, however.

The salesman came back with a teetering tower of shoe boxes—Lanvin, Christian Louboutin, Miu Miu,

Prada—with the huge Balenciaga boot box at the bottom of the stack.

She sat on the couch and tried on the Louboutins first. They had about a five-inch heel and, since Courtney tended to wear only flats, or, if she was feeling really risky, something with a kitten heel, weren't really her style. She would be laughed out of Hawthorne if she showed up in a pair of high-priced hooker shoes, even if they were Louboutins.

Courtney bought the Balenciaga boots. She probably would have bought many more pairs of shoes if Alvero had been there and he could have enjoyed the commission, but she felt too guilty. Guilt was a governing force of Courtney's life. She didn't mind it, though—guilt at least kept her honest.

She had some time to kill, so she strolled around the Meatpacking District and stopped into Stella McCartney, Alexander McQueen, and Carlos Miele. She didn't buy anything. She wasn't in the mood. Courtney suddenly missed Amelia—and His Royal Hotness Zach—a lot. Too much, really. Shopping was just so much more fun with Amelia. Hell, *everything* was just so much more fun with Amelia.

Everything seemed more vibrant and more alive with Amelia around. For instance, if Amelia had been in Jeffrey with Courtney, Amelia would have had something really interesting to say about, like, the history of the shoe buckle in eighteenth-century fashion.

Pastis was a few blocks away, on Ninth Avenue and Gansevoort Street. It was a huge space that was meant, with some success, to look like a Belle Epoque Parisian brasserie—dark wood paneling, flecked antiqued mirrors, and brass sconces on the walls. Courtney bought into the conventional wisdom that held that Balthazar, which was owned by the same guy who owned Pastis, had better food (and much, much better bakery products), but the atmosphere at Pastis was a lot cooler.

As usual, Courtney was ten minutes early to meet Piper and Geoff. She checked in with the maître d' and sat at a stool at the bar. She ordered a virgin Bloody Mary. Courtney knew that this drink choice made her seem like a complete dork—and that Piper would call her on it if she were there, but she didn't care. In St. Bart's she didn't drink, either, but Amelia and Zach never said anything about it. They both drank a fair amount, but neither of them tried to convince Courtney that she should drink too. Amelia and Zach were both so great because they really did seem to accept Courtney as she was. Whereas Piper and Geoff always seemed to try to change her.

"Hey, babe," said a female voice.

Courtney swiveled on her stool.

Piper.

She was decked out from head to foot in Stella McCartney workout clothes. And it wasn't an exaggeration to say *head to foot*: not only was she wearing Stella leggings with leg warmers and a mocha-colored Stella jacket with a number of pockets of superfluous function, but she was also wearing a Stella headband and black Stella athletic shoes.

Piper was probably going down to Equinox on Greenwich Avenue to "work out" after brunch. Actually, Piper never officially worked out—her trips to the gym were made only to meet guys. Older, rich guys.

"What's in the bag?" Piper asked, eyeing Courtney's huge Jeffrey bag.

"Oh, nothing," Courtney said. Suddenly it occurred to her that Piper was going to be offended that she hadn't been invited along on Courtney's mini shopping excursion. "It's just this boring pair of boots I bought."

"Lemme see!" Piper exclaimed. "I want to see! Are they Chloé?"

Courtney could just imagine the scene at the bar at Pastis if she were to take the boots out of the box. Just another spoiled-rotten, pointless Upper East Side schoolgirl showing off her new seven-hundred-dollar shoes, paid for by her parents. Girls like that were a dime a dozen. And *of course* Geoff would just happen to show up right as Courtney was trying to stuff the boots and all the tissue paper wrapping back into the box. How uncool would *that* be?

"I'll show you later," Courtney said. It might not sound like a big deal, but she was proud of standing up for herself, at least this much.

Piper gestured to the bartender.

"Let me get a Bloody Mary here," Piper ordered.

There was a long pause. Courtney thought that the bartender was going to card Piper (how could he not?), but instead he asked, "Is that a *virgin* Bloody Mary, like your friend?"

"Nope," Piper said, giving the bartender a contemptuous look. "Make mine as slutty as possible."

That was Piper. She was, as Courtney's father had often said about her, "a piece of work." Two nights ago, at the Upper East for Lower East event, Courtney got to see Piper in full-on contemptuous mode. At the party, whenever a girl approached Piper, if Piper didn't think the girl was cool enough, or pretty enough, or if she wasn't from the right family, or if—God forbid—her ranking on the stupid socialite website was significantly below Piper's, she would turn on her heel and walk away.

It was always frightening to see Piper cut someone off at her (and it was usually "her") knees. Sometimes Courtney wondered why Piper even bothered with her at all. Courtney hoped it wasn't because her parents had a lot of money.

The bartender banged Piper's Bloody Mary down on the bar.

"Put it on our tab," Piper said.

The maître d' approached them and announced that their table was ready.

As Courtney and Piper, drinks in hand, followed him through Pastis, Courtney was aware of everyone's eyes on her. But maybe it was because of her huge shopping bag, which kept on knocking into everyone's heads.

He led them to a pretty good table at the back, right next to a big end banquette that seated about eight. Courtney threw her bag underneath the table and was getting situated in her chair when Piper started barking out orders again: "We'd rather sit *there*," she said, and pointed to the end banquette. "Can we make this happen?"

Piper had said the exact same thing, in the exact same tone, two nights ago, after the party. As the event was wrapping up (after they had put Courtney's mother and father into their limo and sent them home), Piper decided that she, Courtney, and Geoff were going to go downtown to the Beatrice Inn.

The Beatrice Inn was a superexclusive bar, and Courtney felt that there was no way they were going to be admitted—you had to be Agyness Deyn to get in, and even if you were Agyness Deyn, you still might get turned away. But Piper, as was her habit, alternately charmed, then bullied, the bouncer at the door, and they were let right in.

The Pastis maître d' asked, "How many are in your party?"

"*Three,*" Piper said. "It won't be a problem, I suspect."

"No, it won't be a problem," said the maître d'. "Be my guest." Then he flashed Piper a screw-you grin.

Piper slid into the red banquette, and Courtney sat next to her.

"Did you see the pictures of the party?" asked Piper, then dipped her head down to the straw and sipped at her Bloody Mary.

"I didn't," Courtney said, even though she had. She didn't want anyone knowing that she Google Imaged herself after parties.

"There are so many awesome pictures of me," Piper said. "My Galliano dress was *very* red carpet, don't you think?"

Courtney had to agree that it was.

"And there were a few nice shots of you," Piper said.

Thanks, Piper, Courtney thought. *How generous.*

"Hey, ladies," said a voice. Geoff's. Geoff's voice.

"You're both looking very spry today."

Courtney's heart started pounding, and she could feel the blood pump to her face. She was disappointed about this reaction. She'd hoped that she wouldn't care about Geoff Ellison anymore. Her heart now belonged to Zach Warner. Or at least, she thought it did.

Geoff pulled out the chair from the opposite side of the table. Courtney felt a bit disappointed that Geoff hadn't chosen to sit next to her on the banquette. There was plenty of room. He was wearing a bright orange polo shirt with green appliqué alligators (or crocodiles?) embroidered on the front.

There was no doubt that Geoff was a handsome guy, but his handsomeness couldn't be more unlike the way Zach was handsome. He had green eyes and was as blond and as pale as a ghost (Courtney had overheard some people calling him, derisively, "Casper"), whereas Zach was dark and rugged. Geoff looked like a washed-out picture, Courtney decided; Zach's hotness, on the other hand, had much more of a brooding intensity.

The waiter approached their table and asked for their drink orders. Piper ordered another Bloody Mary, although she wasn't half-finished with the one right in front of her. Courtney ordered a tap water, and Geoff ordered a Bloody Mary, "heavy on the vodka."

"*Tap water!*" Geoff said. "I'm horrified. We've got to

get you to loosen up a little, Courtney."

"*Seriously,*" Piper said, leaning over her straw, "how dorkelicious are you? Why can't you just *live* a little, Court?"

"Did I tell you guys at the party—I can't remember what I told you, I was so wasted—but did I tell you that my parentals are going away the weekend after next to our Hamptons place?"

Both Courtney and Piper responded that he hadn't told them about this development.

"Why don't you guys come and crash and we'll have a huge, insane party?"

"Can't," said Courtney.

Never, did it seem, in Courtney's life had she turned down an invitation from Geoff. It was embarrassing, but she was always around for Geoff whenever he wanted something from her. She was a trophy to be dusted off when needed.

Piper finished off the last of her first Bloody Mary. Then she asked, "Why *can't* you? What *else* do you have going on?"

Courtney resented the implication that she couldn't possibly have something else—something better—to do, and relished the fact that she did. "I'll be in East Hampton. I invited Amelia and Zach out to the house."

"You *what*?" Piper exclaimed. "You've never even

invited *me* out to East Hampton!"

Courtney didn't believe that this was possible—wasn't it *Piper* who was always turning down Courtney's weekend invitations?

"Who are they again?" Geoff asked. "I mean, who are their parents?"

"They're Zach and Amelia Warner," Courtney replied, wondering just how wasted Geoff had been at the party, since she'd told him all about them.

"Never heard of them," said Geoff.

"I've never heard of them, either," said Piper. "What does their father do?"

"He's some big tech guy." As soon as Courtney said this, however, it didn't ring true. Maybe she had misheard what Amelia had said about her father, or misunderstood.

"Where do they go to school?" asked Geoff.

"I think they're going to Brown in August," Courtney said. But now she wasn't sure about that, either. That part, the future part, was all kind of a blur. Maybe that was because Courtney couldn't project beyond the terribly exciting present with Amelia and Zach.

"Why don't we know them?" asked Piper.

"You know that it's Piper's business to know *everyone*," Geoff said.

"They went to boarding schools in Switzerland," Courtney said, "so they're a little bit off the radar."

Their drinks were delivered by the waiter. Piper sucked down almost her entire second Bloody Mary in one go.

"Well, my friend Cecily has been kicked out of just about every boarding school in Switzerland, and she never mentioned these *Warner* people to *me*."

Why did Piper think that she automatically knew every single person in the world? Weren't there, like, six billion people in the world or something? How did Piper expect to know *everyone* within a certain social demographic?

"I'd love for you to meet them," Courtney said, although she kind of liked having them to herself—it was like she had a secret life now, something Geoff and Piper weren't part of at all. Still, she couldn't stop the flow of her words. "I think you guys will really get along."

Piper and Geoff exchanged unsubtle eye rolls.

"I'll text Cecily after lunch and ask her about these mysterious Warners," said Piper.

"You should," Courtney said, annoyed, but pretending not to be. "I'm sure you'll find out all sorts of wonderful things about them."

"I'm *sure*," Piper said ominously. "I'm sure they'll turn out to be *world-class*."

Ugh. Courtney wished she'd just kept her secret life to herself.

10

Escape to New York

TUESDAY AFTERNOON, VESPASIAN, NH

Could the sleepy town of Vespasian, New Hampshire, *be* any sleepier? Just driving back into town and seeing the sign that welcomed them to Vespasian (THE LITTLE TOWN THAT TIME FORGOT) made Amelia want to pass out and become a vegetable forevermore.

There was *nothing* to do in Vespasian. It was the kind of town that was referred to as "charming" and "leafy" in AAA guidebooks. "Charming" was always a euphemism for "small," and it didn't get any smaller than Vespasian: one tree-lined main street (called not "Main Street," but "Market Street"—yes, Vespasian sure knew how to mix it up), with one restaurant, one bar, one store that sold expensive clothing for animals, and numerous stores that sold candles, potpourri, and wind chimes. That was it. That was the town. The nearest drug store was twenty-five minutes away, and the nearest liquor store was forty minutes away.

Amelia and Zach's father didn't seem to understand why his children were so bored in Vespasian. "Go for a walk in the woods! Become one with nature!" he would exclaim whenever Amelia flung herself onto the couch, complaining that she was so bored that she could literally feel her brain leaking out of her ears. But her father's suggestions only made her more bored and depressed, because anyone who really knew Amelia at all would know that she wasn't an outdoorsy girl. She would rather take a hundred trig classes than go for one hike in the woods, and she was *really* bad at trig.

Not only was Vespasian, New Hampshire, the lamest of all the towns they'd lived in, but their apartment was the worst of anywhere they'd lived too. In the past they had always rented cool houses in various states of disrepair, but now they were renting this totally dubious three-bedroom apartment over a store on Market Street. The old wood floors were slanted, and the walls buckled, and most of the windows were painted shut and wouldn't open. The bathroom didn't even have a bathtub, but a sad little shower stall that you had to stand up in, and the kitchen didn't have a real stove. It had—*oh, God*—a *hot plate*!

The only good thing about the apartment was that it was on the second floor, above one of those ubiquitous candle/potpourri stores, which meant that it always smelled nice. And you could tell what season it was by how their apartment smelled, since the store downstairs changed its scents according to the time of year. In the spring their apartment had smelled of lilies and lilacs; around Valentine's Day, roses; and at Christmas, pine needles, chestnuts, and cinnamon.

Today Amelia had noticed that the scent had changed. She sniffed and decided that vanilla must mean summer, which bummed her out. Vanilla was too sweet, too strong. She'd hoped for something clean and crisp, like cucumber or lavender. "Don't you wish we were still in St. Bart's, Dad?"

Her dad was sitting in the front room in his old cracked leather club chair, illuminated by a brass floor lamp. The Oriental rug on the floor was threadbare, but you couldn't really see much of the rug (or what was left of the rug) through all of her father's ancient *New Yorkers* scattered across it.

"When we were in St. Bart's, you wanted to come home. Now that we're finally home, you want to go back? You must subscribe to Emerson's belief that 'a foolish consistency is the hobgoblin of little minds.'"

"What's the difference between a 'foolish' consistency and an 'unfoolish' consistency?"

Her father took off his glasses and pressed one of the arms to his lips in a thoughtful, professorial gesture.

"You've always been too smart by half, haven't you, Ann?"

Not really. If Amelia had been too smart by half, then would she really be here, in this cramped, horrible, tragic little apartment? If she were twice as smart (or half as smart—what did "by half" mean?), wouldn't she be hanging out with Courtney Moore at Pastis (Courtney had texted her from brunch on Monday), and having the paparazzi take her picture as she and Courtney were hailing a cab, pictures that would then be put up on celebrity websites?

"Dad?" Amelia asked, "can we go into Concord tonight for dinner?"

Concord was the biggest city around, which wasn't saying much, but, like, at least it was a *metropolis.* Sort of. Amelia was, like every country bumpkin who'd gotten a taste of cosmopolitan life, desperate for a tiny glimpse of glamour right now.

"Ann, you know I have a dinner at the department chair's house tonight," her father said wearily.

Oh yeah. Amelia remembered now. (She'd given up on getting her dad to call her Amelia; he was having none of it.) And Zach was out playing basketball with some friends. So she was on her own for tonight.

"Okay. I guess I'll just go into my room and die now," she said.

"Don't be so histrionic. Why don't you read a book or do something useful?"

"Don't worry about me," Amelia said, trying to lay on the self-pity. "I guess I'll just make mac and cheese on the hot plate, and eat it in my room."

A few hours later Amelia was alone. She had already flipped through every single magazine in the apartment, except for her father's *New Yorkers*, which bored her to tears, and she hated TV. She decided not to make mac and cheese, because making food meant making dirty dishes, and she hated doing dishes more than she hated doing anything else in the world except possibly hiking in the woods.

The only good news about having all this time to kill was that she got to play with her new makeup that she'd ordered from the Sephora website while she was in St. Bart's, during those boring days after Courtney had left. The package from Sephora was waiting for her downstairs at the candle store (the lady at the candle store always signed for the Warners' deliveries) upon their return. She'd ordered about ten tubes of DiorShow mascara, in different colors (the blue had been a stupid idea—what was she thinking?), and three different tubes of Chanel lipstick.

But the real splurges in the box had been a two-ounce jar of Crème de la Mer and a big bottle of Frédéric Fekkai shampoo. Amelia's dad was going to *freak* when he got his credit card statement in a couple of weeks. She wasn't looking forward to that day, but at least her new products would keep her beautiful until that day arrived.

But no matter how beautiful she was, she was still bored. It was funny: even if you were beautiful, and encased in hundreds of dollars' worth of lotion, you could still be bored and unhappy.

Amelia's room had posters of the Sex Pistols and Rudolf Nureyev in it—both Johnny Rotten and Rudy being big heroes of hers. The main point of interest in the room, though, was a huge gilt mirror. It was one of the biggest mirrors she'd ever seen, and she was looking at her reflection in it.

She was wearing all three shades of her new Chanel lipsticks at once, and was completely slathered in Crème de la Mer when she decided to make a phone call. No, not to her new BFF Courtney Moore, but to her uncle Mike, who wasn't really her uncle, but . . . well, it was complicated.

Uncle Mike was an important person in Amelia's life for a number of reasons. The first reason: he lived in Manhattan, and was always ready for offering up his apartment whenever Amelia and Zach needed a crash pad. The other, less imperative reason for his significance in her life: he was Amelia's voice of reason, the person she always went to for practical advice, since whatever advice her father had to give her had nothing to do with the real world. Plus, Mike was like a magician, the kind who could turn, say, an ugly but expensive bracelet that was supposedly some kind of family heirloom into a wad of cash.

Mike was thirtyish, and was known to be a former "business partner" of their mother's, before she left them forever ten years ago. Neither Amelia nor Zach knew what "business partner" meant, since as far as they knew their mother had been, like, a professional personal assistant to some rich old man, but they had never pressed Uncle Mike for further details. Honestly, Amelia and Zach probably didn't want to know.

Amelia did know a little bit about Uncle Mike's background, but what she knew was painted with a very broad brush. He was a former runaway, and when he was a kid, a couple years younger than Amelia was now, her mother apparently took him in. Amelia's mother became, in a way, his surrogate mother. It must have been some sort of vestigial loyalty that made him always available to Amelia and Zach, and always ready to take them under his wing.

She could have pressed her father for information about Uncle Mike, but her father sort of didn't know that

Amelia and Zach had any contact with him. Their father had detached himself completely from their mother and everyone and everything associated with her. He wouldn't have approved if he knew that Amelia frequently called Uncle Mike for life advice. And he doubly wouldn't have approved if he knew that Amelia and Zach stayed in Uncle Mike's apartment when they visited the city; their father still believed that they stayed with friends of Amelia's, friends from one of her many schools, for their Manhattan sojourns.

As if Amelia had any real friends.

Amelia's hands were so slick from the Crème de la Mer that her phone kept slipping out of her hands as she was trying to punch in Uncle Mike's speed-dial number. He picked up on the second ring. One of the good things about Uncle Mike was that he was always there.

"Yo, Amelia, 'sup?"

It was very noisy in the background. Uncle Mike was definitely not at home. But who could blame him? He lived in a minuscule studio apartment in Hell's Kitchen, and didn't seem to spend too much time there.

"Hey, there, my uncle. Where *are* you? I can barely hear you."

"Oh, I'm just out with my, uh, *associates.*"

She decided not to ask Uncle Mike who his "associates" were.

"Let me step outside where I can hear you better," he said.

The din of a closed room (a bar? a pool hall?) was replaced by street noise, which meant lots of sirens and honking horns.

"How are you, Amelia? Did you and Zach stay out of trouble in St. Bart's like I told you to?"

She liked Uncle Mike because he called her Amelia and not Ann, like her father did. When *Zach* deigned to call her Amelia, it looked as if the act of forming the word in his mouth caused him great physical pain.

"It was pretty awesome. We went to that place Le Ti, like you said. We *loved* it."

"Cool. Was my favorite belly dancer, Ciela, there? Did you tell her Mike said hi?"

Amelia had forgotten to look for a certain belly dancer—tawny, one hundred and ten pounds—and give her Uncle Mike's regards.

She lied and said that she did locate this Ciela. "She told me to tell you to come and see her sometime," Amelia said.

"That's cool." He paused. "So. What else is going on with you? What can I do you for?"

It seemed kind of sad that Uncle Mike thought that Amelia called him only when she wanted something. Which was basically true, although she preferred not to think of their relationship that way.

"I've got a question to ask you," Amelia said. She looked at herself in the mirror. The blue mascara wasn't really all that bad. From certain lights, it actually looked plum colored. "Do you think it would be possible for us to stay with you in the city for a few days?"

It was always a blast staying with Uncle Mike, although Amelia really didn't care for the neighborhood, even though it was supposed to be one of the up-and-coming areas of the city. He would buy beer for them, and he always had cigarettes lying around his apartment. And when he caught them smoking, he wouldn't make them put their cigarettes out, but would instead teach them how to blow smoke rings.

More important, she needed to get herself back into Courtney Moore's world, before Courtney forgot about her entirely. Amelia had seen the pictures of Courtney with Piper and Geoff at the Upper East for Lower East party, and she certainly looked happy enough without Amelia. Of course Amelia was excited about the invitation to the Hamptons, but that was a whole week and a half away! In that time, someone else could come in and try to lure Courtney into her evil clutches.

"Well," Uncle Mike said. There was a really loud siren in the background. "I'm actually heading out of town for a few days, so I don't—"

"Even better!" said Amelia. "Zach and I can house-sit for you." Or room-sit, Amelia thought, given the size of Mike's place. Still, at least it wasn't Vespasian, New Hampshire!

"You want me to leave you all alone in the big, bad city? I don't know. . . . "

"Oh, c'mon," Amelia said. "I think we can handle it."

"And can I ask why the trip now to the isle of Manhattos?"

Manhattos? Maybe that was what the original Native Americans called Manhattan? Uncle Mike was always saying crazy, off-the-wall stuff like that.

"I'm coming to see my new friend, Courtney Moore!" She was barely able to control her excitement, or her pride at being able to call herself a friend of Courtney Moore's. In addition to all her other good qualities, Courtney really was a good person. And there weren't many of those left these days, not many at all.

"Am I supposed to know who this Courtney chick is?"

"Oh, you will," Amelia said, scooping about a hundred dollars' worth of Crème de la Mer onto her hands.

"Sure I will," Mike said.

Amelia resented the patronizing tone in Mike's voice and felt a little wounded by it even, but she ignored it, because the next thing he said was exactly what she wanted to hear: "Of course you can crash here."

11

Friends Don't Let Friends Live in Construction Zones

WEDNESDAY AFTERNOON, NEW YORK

Summer in the city was kind of boring and hot, and Courtney understood now why most people they knew went to the Vineyard, or the Hamptons, or Maine, or Nova Scotia (randomly, Nova Scotia was the new cool place to buy a vacation house). When Courtney was younger, she and her parents used to go down to the Jersey Shore. As a vacation it wasn't glamorous or luxe, but she hadn't been interested in glamour or luxury at that point in her life. She and her father would go out to the beach and make sand castles, and Courtney would stand on her father's feet when they went in the water.

It seemed sad to Courtney that she could never get those innocent days back.

Now everything seemed so much more complicated, Courtney thought as she lay on her Frette duvet and stared up at the ceiling. Her father had left this morning for Brazil—he had some meeting he had to attend in São Paulo. And Courtney's mother was off for a day of grooming—nails, facial, Botox, eyebrow shaping—before her board meeting tonight at the New York Philharmonic. If her mother had some big event at night, she would try to arrange for "a day of beauty" (as she called it) beforehand. It was amazing how much time and effort it seemed to take for her to feel like she looked halfway decent. (Courtney wondered if her mother filled her days with such trivial tasks because she didn't have enough to do now that she'd stopped working.)

The mothers of everyone else she knew (especially Piper's and Geoff's mothers) were all very well put-together ladies, but Courtney did wonder if all of them spent as much time and money at it as her own mother did. And what about Amelia and Zach's mother? Was she vain too, like all the rest of them?

Amelia and Zach had never actually mentioned their mother, and Courtney got the feeling that it was none of her business to bring her up. Was their mother still alive? Was she still married to Amelia and Zach's father?

Was she even around at all?

Courtney heard someone milling about in the hallway and knew that it would be Nabby, the housekeeper who came every afternoon to clean, shop, and make dinner for Courtney and her parents.

Courtney stood up to greet her. She was a tall woman with an angular face. She always wore her hair in a tight bun, and Courtney wondered if she wore it that way in her regular life too, or if it was just part of her housekeeper persona.

"Hey, Nabby," Courtney said, leaning against her now-open door and fiddling with the crystal knob. "How are you today?"

"I'm good, sweetheart. Just wanted to see if you needed anything at the store."

Every day Nabby asked, and every day Courtney had Nabby get her the same things: Diet Coke, Butter Rum Life Savers, and Extra gum, Bubblemint flavor.

"Just the usual, thanks, Nabby," Courtney said.

"Life Savers, soda, and gum. Got it."

Courtney felt so predictable. Why was she so boring and predictable?

"Oh, and can you get a treat for Peekaboo?"

Peekaboo, their beloved dog, seemed really bored and mopey, and had spent the whole day lying like a bum on the parlor couch. Courtney thought that maybe a treat would cheer her up.

She remembered back to the days when they lived in the East Village—it seemed as if her mother had spent a third of her life at the grocery store, another third cooking what she had bought at the grocery store, and the last third at the shop she ran. Her mother hadn't done any of those things for five years, since they moved to the Upper East Side.

Courtney sat on the big velvet dusky rose–colored couch by her bedroom window, and she was thinking now about Zach's skin. It had been fun watching Zach's skin get darker and darker during their time together in St. Bart's. He was such a beautiful, exotic caramel color.

She pulled back the heavy taffeta drapes and gazed down at the green expanse of Central Park, and thought about how nice it would be to share this view with Zach. If you opened the window and craned your head all the way to the right, you could even see the grand white colossus of the Metropolitan Museum of Art. If Zach were here, they could almost pretend they were together in Rome.

How nice it would be to travel with Zach someday.

Over on her Regency desk, her phone rang. She skipped over to it, and her heart leaped when she saw the name on the caller ID.

"Are your ears burning?" Courtney asked. "I was just thinking about you and Zach!"

"Really?" Amelia said. "What were you thinking?"

"That I'm bored beyond belief and I wish you guys were here," Courtney said.

"Then this is your lucky day!"

"You're in the city?!"

"We went to our house in Palm Beach for a few days after St. Bart's, but I couldn't wait to get out of there," Amelia said. "Don't you just *detest* Palm Beach? I mean, the wealth is so conspicuous there. I read *The Theory of the Leisure Class* by Thorstein Veblen just to keep myself sane. Have you ever read it?"

Courtney had to admit that she hadn't.

"It was one of the first critiques of consumerism ever written, and Veblen argues that people waste all this money only so that they can be seen as higher status by other people in their group. You can't be in Palm Beach and not think of his term 'conspicuous consumption.' Zach and I were practically *begging* my father to sell his Rolls-Royce when we were down there."

"Is *Zach* in the city with you?"

It was impossible for her to mention Zach's name without emphasizing it in some way. The very act of saying his name made Courtney feel special. But if she wasn't careful, she was going to give herself away. . . .

"No, I'm afraid not," Amelia said. "He's in Paris, meeting with the president, Nicolas Sarkozy. He works for him, you know."

Jesus. That was possibly the most impressive summer job Courtney had ever heard of. What made it even more impressive was the fact that Zach had never mentioned an interest in politics, nor had Courtney noticed Zach speaking French when they were in St. Bart's, and *everyone* spoke French in St. Bart's. But this was one of the things Courtney liked best about Zach: his modesty.

Still, though, Courtney was bummed that Zach wasn't with Amelia.

"When is he coming back?" Courtney asked. She hoped that question didn't seem too desperate.

"Well, he's starting at Yale in the fall, so he's abroad for a couple months."

"I thought you said he was going to Brown?"

"Oh *yeahhhh*," Amelia said. "He got into *both* places, but he just made his final decision when we were in Palm Beach. We were as shocked as you are. The education at Brown is *so* much finer."

On the contrary: Courtney was quite pleased by this information; New Haven was only an hour and a half from New York by Amtrak. Two years ago she had done a summer program for a couple of weeks at Yale, and she found the trip surprisingly painless. It sucked to think about him being so far away for the rest of the summer, but it was delightful to contemplate that he would be a train ride away in August.

"Did your dad come back with you?" Courtney asked.

"No. Dad had to go to Panama to work on this huge project with the turnover of the canal."

Courtney had no idea what Amelia was talking about, but she didn't let on.

"I'm all alone in our apartment," Amelia continued, "and it's a nightmare, *believe me*—all this construction!"

Courtney knew all about the nightmare of apartment construction. When her parents bought this place on the Upper East Side, they actually bought all three apartments on the twelfth floor of the building. The entire first year they lived here, the whole area was a construction zone, and everything in Courtney's life was coated in a fine film of sawdust. (That year she even tasted sawdust whenever she ate her dinner.)

It also seemed that there were always random burly men stomping through their apartment in their filthy work boots, often smoking cigarettes and using her family's floors as their ashtrays. Her dad had considered moving them all to a sublet for a while, but then decided it would be a waste of money, although she and her mother did stay at the Carlyle Hotel a few times when things got especially messy and her dad was out of town. Courtney's mother still talked about, with a shudder, the condition of their bathrooms during that year, after the workmen had gotten through with them.

You would have thought that knocking the walls down in three apartments and making one huge apartment would have been a fairly simple procedure, but that had not been the case.

"I totally sympathize with you," Courtney said. "We had a similar thing done to our apartment."

"What?" Amelia asked.

"Oh, it's stupid," Courtney said. And then she remembered what Amelia had said about that book, *The Theory of the Leisure Class.* "My parents bought all three units on the floor and made them into one big apartment. Have you ever heard of such an example of conspicuous consumption?"

"Oh my God, that is so crazy!" Amelia said. "Because we're knocking down *four* apartments! Isn't it so bizarre that we're doing the same thing?"

Courtney was sad that Amelia and Zach had to go through the supreme annoyance of construction work . . . but it was nice to think that Zach would someday get to ramble around (without a shirt!) his own private wing of the apartment. . . .

A thought occurred to Courtney.

"You know what, Amelia?"

"What, Courtney?"

"You and Zach should really consider staying with us when you're in the city."

"Oh, we could never impose," Amelia said.

"No, I mean it. We would love to have you. My parents *adored* you and Zach."

"Gee whiz," Amelia said. "I mean, that's so supernice of you! Maybe we—I mean, I, since Zach is in Paris—could take you up on that. But you know what they say about fish and guests: after three days, they stink."

Courtney didn't know that, but whatever. "Do you think you could come over *tonight*?"

Courtney was getting all excited, because they had three guest rooms, and Amelia could have her pick. Courtney sort of assumed that Amelia would choose the French Empire–style room, but the Japanese bedroom with the koi garden was also really nice, as was the sleek, modern room all done in white.

She should run this by her mother, Courtney thought, although she was pretty sure having Amelia here wouldn't be a problem. Their apartment was so monstrous that her mother probably wouldn't even notice!

"I have to tell you, Courtney," Amelia said, "this is just about the nicest thing anyone has ever done for me. We *must* go out tonight and celebrate!"

Courtney's mother wouldn't be back until at least midnight, so the chances were that Courtney—and

Amelia—would get back while her mother was still out.

"Let's go to Buddakan, and then the Beatrice Inn! Unless you'd rather go to Del Posto."

"That sounds awesome," Courtney said.

"Which?" Amelia asked. "Buddakan or Del Posto?"

"Totally up to you," Courtney said. The real pleasure tonight would be being with Amelia. Courtney didn't care about what kind of *food* they ate, although she did love Buddakan. It was much more pleasant to make a plan with Amelia than it was to make a plan with Piper. Piper was so aggressive and bossy about everything, whereas with Amelia every decision was a choice. And it was almost as if Amelia were sort of magically *intuiting* what Courtney wanted to do.

"Buddakan. Okay. So I'm packing a bag right now," Amelia said.

"Where's Razzmatazz?" asked Courtney. "You're welcome to bring him over here. He and Peekaboo could have a playdate!"

"Aww," Amelia said. "Thanks. But Razzy's out at the country house for the summer. What do you think we should wear tonight? Do you have any Prada from the new fall collection?"

Courtney had to think about that for a second.

Yes, in fact, she did have a couple of dresses and a sweater. Before they left for St. Bart's her mother had taken her to Bergdorf Goodman, where they started their fall shopping.

"Yeah, I do. Never worn," Courtney said.

"Great," Amelia replied. "Because I'd love to wear Prada fall tonight."

Courtney had never had a friend with whom she shared clothes before. It just went to show how close they were getting, and how special their relationship was becoming.

12

Everybody's Working for the Weekend

FRIDAY MORNING, VESPASIAN, NH

Zach's lunch break hadn't come soon enough. He had hoped that he wouldn't have to come back to his job as a handyman at their lame private school in Vespasian after their trip to St. Bart's, but it hadn't worked out that way. St. Bart's had used up every cent Zach had made at the school his first couple of weeks on the job, so he had to do something . . . although Amelia, of course, didn't have to have a job (she never needed one). It was probably a certain inertia that drew him back here—the job was waiting for him, and it was always easier to go back to a job that was waiting for you than it was to go out and actually look for a new one.

The work was superboring and brainless—he had spent his entire day cutting frames and matting, and cleaning glass. The school decided they wanted to reframe every single picture on the wall, and Zach got the honor. He had learned only one thing today: regular old water was a better glass cleaner than Windex.

There'd probably been worse jobs in the history of the world, because at least he got to listen to his iPod at work. But it did piss him off that his sister was allowed to be jobless and idle all summer long. It was like his dad was willfully ignorant about how his daughter spent her summer vacation.

Zach ate his lunches in an empty classroom. He brought the same thing to lunch every day from home—a box of Lunchables (ham and cheddar, natch), a huge bottle of Sprite, and a York peppermint patty. It was good to not have to think about what you were going to eat at lunch, although it was kind of boring too. The other thing about the Lunchables was that they had so much sodium in them that Zach felt like a prune for the rest of the day.

Zach still had ten minutes until he had to get back to work, so he decided to make the most of that time by calling his sister. Amelia was in New York, staying with Courtney. The fact that she was shacking up with

Courtney meant that it was just Zach and his dad alone in the apartment. As much as his sister was capable of irritating the hell out of him, Zach did miss her when she wasn't around. She definitely made things more exciting at home, even if most of her summer so far had been spent lounging around their apartment and complaining about how "dismal and unglamorous" everything in Vespasian was (not that that kind of attitude wasn't a constant for Amelia).

He punched Amelia's number on speed dial. She answered on the first ring.

"Hello, little brother. How are you?"

"You'd better be careful and keep your lies straight, Ann. You don't want Courtney to overhear. I thought we were supposed to be *twins*."

"Zachary Warner, you are *sooooo* naive. Do you know how many square feet the Moores' apartment is? Besides, I'm an entire twenty-five minutes older than you, let's not forget."

Zach thought about the square-footage question for a moment. Their own apartment in town over the candle store was about eight hundred square feet, but their apartment was in New Hampshire, where real estate prices were way cheaper than in Manhattan, so eight hundred square feet would actually be a pretty decent-size apartment there. But, again, the Moores were rich, so multiply it by three.

"Twenty-four hundred square feet," Zach said.

"Wrong!" Amelia said. "It's nine thousand square feet! Their apartment is so big that I can scream that from the top of my lungs: *Nine thousand square feet! I have three whole rooms to myself!*"

Zach was overcome with a pang of jealousy. He wanted to be there too, in Courtney's apartment, in Courtney's life, but he hadn't been invited in.

"We've been having the *best* time, Zachary. We went to Buddakan, then the Beatrice Inn, and yesterday we had lunch at the restaurant on the sixth floor of Bergdorf Goodman; then we had drinks at the Café Carlyle. Well, Courtney didn't drink anything other than tap water, but she bought me a bottle of Dom Pérignon from *1998*! Can you believe it? Do you understand what that means? Nineteen ninety-eight: the best year *ever*! She's not shy about throwing her parents' money around."

Zach was dying to ask whether Courtney had said anything about him. If Amelia were a normal person, she would have brought up the topic herself and spared Zach the embarrassment: *Courtney is talking nonstop about you. Courtney likes you.* But no. That wasn't Amelia. Something so straightforward would be too easy, and too sane.

"Can I ask you why you think Courtney Moore has

taken such an interest in you?" Zach asked.

"*Zachary*," Amelia responded, "can you not see that Courtney and I are soul mates? Last night at the Café Carlyle, during intermission—this old lady sang show tunes, but it was still pretty awesome—it got sooooo heavy. Courtney told me that it was like we shared a brain and a heart."

A brain and a heart? *Barf.* Were they *dating*?

"And do you feel that way too?"

"Of course," Amelia said. "As much as a mastermind can. You know, I can't get too emotionally involved."

"Mastermind?" Zach asked.

Zach ripped open his peppermint patty wrapper and broke the candy in half. Then he broke it in half again and popped one of the quartered pieces into his mouth.

"And you're a mastermind of what again?" he asked.

One of the things he loved—and hated—about his sister was her arrogance. She seriously believed she *was* some kind of mastermind. Someone who had a more realistic view of herself really wouldn't treat people the way Amelia—Ann—was always treating people.

It made Zach kind of sick to think about his sister's sordid history with both girls and guys. She used people. She was a user of people. Amelia had an uncanny ability to determine immediately what made someone special, and then she went about trying to steal that special thing.

And when Amelia had stolen what she wanted to steal, she promptly dropped that person. It was an awful thing to watch. She had hurt a lot of people.

"I am a mastermind," Amelia said, enunciating grandly, "of *charm.*"

Well, if charm meant getting inside someone's head and repeating that person's thoughts back to her, then Amelia had it in spades. She was a good actress, and she had an uncanny ability to imitate people's speech patterns and mannerisms. At the end of the trip to St. Bart's—well, at the end of *Courtney's* part of the trip—Zach noticed that his insane sister was flinging her hair back and pursing her lips the same exact way that Courtney did.

And what painfully gorgeous hair and lips Courtney had . . .

"Well, I'm glad you're having such an awesome time," Zach said. "Maybe I'll get out to New York one of these days." He uttered that sentence in a tone of self-pity. Would his sister pick up on it?

"Zachary, I need to tell you something," Amelia said. Her voice was softer now, quieter, almost conspiratorial. "Courtney is totally in love with you."

Zach couldn't believe what he was hearing. Literally: he couldn't believe what he was hearing, because Amelia often lied when it suited her purposes.

"For real?"

"Totally. She talks about you all the time, and I don't get the feeling that she's a girl who talks about guys, like, ever. You should come to New York and stay here."

Had Amelia forgotten that Zach was sort of otherwise *occupied*? As in, he had a *job*. It must have been nice to be Amelia, to not have to live off what she had earned at some stupid summer job, but instead rely on the kindness of others.

God, Amelia was becoming so much like their mother it was scary. The last thing Uncle Mike told them about their mother was that she was living at the Hôtel de Crillon in Paris, as some rich old perv's mistress. No wonder Amelia sometimes preferred to pretend she was dead.

"I do have a job, you know, Ann," Zach said.

"Why don't you blow it off tomorrow and come here tonight? Courtney was just talking about how you could have the Koi Room if you came. Can you believe that all of the guest rooms are named?"

"I guess I could call in sick tomorrow."

Taking a sick day probably wouldn't go over too well with Mr. Peters, the head maintenance guy. Mr. Peters was still pissed at Zach for taking off two weeks to go to St. Bart's and had only said it was okay after Zach agreed to work a few Saturdays. When Zach told him where he was going on vacation, Mr. Peters seemed to take great joy in telling him that he had never once been out of the country, and hadn't left the great state of New Hampshire for over twenty years. To Zach, that boast was like, *Kill me now.*

"Please, please, please, please, please come out!" Amelia said. Their father hated it when she begged, and told her that such behavior reminded him too much of their mother. That would shut Amelia up quick. She worshiped and hated their mother equally, but she also seemed to have a fear that she might become like her someday.

It was funny to Zach that Amelia couldn't see that had already happened.

"I wouldn't mind seeing Courtney, I guess," Zach said, trying to sound casual. He could, he supposed, take the bus from Concord to New York later in the evening.

"Oh, but there's one thing that I should tell you," Amelia said.

"Uh-oh," Zach said.

"Uh-oh what? It's just that I sort of told Courtney you had a summer job in France working for the president."

"The president of *what*?" Zach asked.

"The president of France," Amelia said.

You never knew what lies Amelia was going to come up with. No matter what she concocted, it was always a surprise. But couldn't she have come up with a more *believable* fib this time? Even the lies she'd told some random couple they'd met in St. Bart's on their first day about how he had won three Olympic gold medals for downhill skiing seemed somehow more plausible.

"What if Courtney starts talking French with me?" Zach asked, panicked. All rich, sophisticated, cultured people like Courtney were fluent in French, weren't they? Zach didn't know a lick of French—he'd studied Spanish for three years, and still couldn't string a coherent sentence together.

"If she speaks French with you it's only because it's the language of love. If she does, just grab her and start making out. She totally wants you, I'm telling you."

Every time he heard Amelia say this, it made him believe it just a little bit more. With Amelia it was often impossible to tell the lies from the truth. But sometimes it really was in your own best interest to believe what she told you.

In this case, he would pretend that his only sister was telling the truth.

"I'll pack my bag tonight," Zach said.

"Could you grab my Lanvin flats while you're at it?" Amelia asked.

Zach could feel his blood starting to boil. Sometimes even the most innocuous things that his sister said pissed him off.

"Are you only inviting me to New York because you want me to bring your *shoes*?"

"When did you get so cynical, Zachary? You should learn to be all innocent, peaceful, and Zen. Like me."

Sure, Zach thought, *that's just what I want to be: like you.*

13

How to Eavesdrop Like a Lady

FRIDAY MORNING, NEW YORK

Amelia got off the phone with Zach and swanned around her room in Courtney's apartment. *Apartment* seemed too small-minded a word for the extreme luxury of the massive Moore home. In Amelia's life she had seen some pretty swank mansions, but Courtney's home, if it wasn't as big as the Radziwill estate in Palm Beach, was definitely better appointed.

She bent over and picked up Peekaboo, drawing the dog to her chest, and smiled at herself (and Peekaboo) in the mirror. She bowed, pretending she was at a ball. A classy little Cavalier King Charles spaniel like Peekaboo would be the perfect party accessory for a glamour girl like Amelia, she thought.

The room was as grand and lavish as the state apartments in the Palace of Versailles. There was a chandelier; and three marble fireplaces, each with a bust of a different white dude in a wig; and the walls were covered with ornate gold tapestries depicting hunt scenes and naked goddesses. The view outside the full-length windows was of the calming green of Central Park. It was Amelia's dream view, and it was Amelia's dream room.

Amelia could totally see herself living here, at least for a while. The only problem was, her dad definitely wouldn't go for it, and neither, probably, would Zach. But maybe Zach could move in too. Courtney would second that plan, Amelia felt sure.

She hated to admit this, but Courtney's growing interest in Zach, and Zach's growing interest in Courtney, made her feel kind of jealous. She knew that it was immature of her to feel this way, because her bond with Courtney was so strong already, but in the back of her mind was a nagging fear that, if the two of them got heavy, then she would be left out. She hated the idea of being a third wheel. Being a third wheel didn't suit her—never would. Anyway, it was a tricky situation with Courtney and Zach, because Amelia needed them to be close.

That idea made Amelia's motives sound sinister, when

they weren't at all! She actually was growing quite fond of shy, dorky, beautiful, rich Courtney. And befriending Courtney had another subsidiary benefit too: Courtney seemed so happy just spending time with Amelia, which made Amelia feel pretty great about herself.

But here was another thing that was eating her up: Why had Zach just been such a jerk on the phone? He had a real chip on his shoulder about his summer job at their fantastically depressing school, and he seemed quietly—or not so quietly, really—resentful that she didn't have to have one. Amelia understood, in a way, why Zach was mad at her for not working, but Amelia had her own way of making money. And it wasn't like cozying up to rich people wasn't *work.* Making Courtney Moore feel as if she were Amelia's soul mate, as if she were the only person who mattered in the entire world, *was* a job, in a way.

There was something else in Zach's tone that bothered Amelia too—she felt a certain disapproving undercurrent in everything he had said on the phone. He could get like this sometimes—he seemed to love to believe that he was morally superior to her. (Yeah, right. As if Amelia hadn't witnessed some of the truly awful stuff Zach had done before.) So, as much as she loved her little brother, Amelia really hated feeling judged by him. It was as if he believed that she was dragging him down into an amoral morass with her.

Also, she hated it when Zach called her Ann. He did that just to bug her.

If they had had enough money to go to a family therapist, Amelia would like to talk about this. Because she didn't believe that she was a bad person. She had just been screwed over a lot already in her life, and she deserved to have things evened out at least a little bit.

There were voices in the adjacent room. (It was surprising that the sound traveled through the thick walls, and now Amelia was wishing she hadn't been yelling before—she hoped no one had been near enough to hear her.) Amelia recognized Courtney's voice, of course, but there was another unfamiliar female voice. It wasn't Courtney's mother, because Amelia would recognize Mrs. Moore's voice, and also because this voice was younger.

Amelia put the dog down on the bed. She wondered vaguely if Peekaboo was allowed on the bed, but decided not to concern herself with such details.

She pressed her ear to the door.

"I totally can't wait for you to meet her!" said the muffled voice of Courtney. "You're going to *love* each other."

"Yeah, I know. You've said that, like, a million times."

It was Piper. Piper Hansen. The hottest young socialite in New York, and, according to *New York* magazine, the most beautiful. (Although Amelia disagreed with that opinion: She believed that *she*, Amelia Warner, was the most beautiful. The sucky thing was that no one knew who Amelia was. *Yet.*)

"I talked to Cecily this morning, and she had never heard of any Warner twins. Where did you say they went to school again?"

OMG. Piper was talking about Amelia and Zach. How *dare* she? How dare she try to pry into their pasts! Amelia found herself hating Piper already, even though she hadn't met her yet. (Although Amelia couldn't help but be flattered, a little bit, that Piper was talking about her.)

"Shhhh," Courtney said. "She's in the room right next door, and she might be able to hear you."

"*Courtney,*" Piper said. "How much did your parents pay for this apartment? Twenty million? We all still remember the piece from the *Times.* Let's *hope* that the walls are a little thicker than cardboard. And *why* is this girl staying here again?"

Amelia wanted to bust her fist right through the surprisingly thin wall and wring Piper's swanlike neck. What a wench! Why had she chosen poor little sad Amelia Warner, whose mother ran away from home when she was a child, and who had never been given one thing in her entire godforsaken life, to pick on?

She wasn't exactly predisposed to like Piper already, even under the best conditions. Courtney talked about Piper—and that guy Geoff, from the Upper East for Lower East charity pictures—only occasionally, but even occasionally was too much for Amelia. Amelia felt that she was beginning to understand things about Courtney's relationship with Piper—Piper was loud and bold and bossy, and was definitely the alpha in their friendship.

It seemed that Courtney had more conflicted feelings about Piper than she did about Amelia. (With Amelia and Courtney, it was all roses and sunshiny days all the time.) Amelia felt, from the tension in Courtney's voice whenever she talked about Piper, that Piper was really competitive with her, and was always trying to undermine her and everyone else. Amelia liked to make Courtney feel better about herself, whereas Piper seemed to like to make Courtney feel worse.

Long story short: Piper didn't seem like a very nice person, and Amelia wasn't looking forward to meeting her. No way.

"Her father is having work done on their apartment—it's a *total* nightmare," Courtney was saying. "And we're trying to get Zach to come back early from Paris so he can stay here too!"

"Paris?"

Amelia didn't care for Piper's snotty tone. She said *Paris* as if it were something disgusting that she had to spit out of her mouth.

On the bed, Peekaboo wagged her feathery red tail.

"He's working for the president of France! Isn't that amazing?"

"Wait. How old are they again?"

Oh no! Piper was asking way too many questions. *Where* did she get off? One of the many great things about Courtney was that she didn't ask too many questions. She was so sweet and innocent that she seemed to take everything that Amelia said on faith. It was very refreshing, actually. Everyone Amelia met always seemed so cynical and bitter (not unlike Piper); never before had she met someone who was as willing to believe as Courtney.

Gullible was a much less nice word to describe what Courtney was.

"They're a little bit older," Courtney said, and Amelia could tell Courtney felt cool having "older" friends. "They're eighteen. Or seventeen. I can't remember."

"Courtney, my dear trembling rosebud, have you ever heard of an eighteen-year-old who had a job working for the president of *France*?"

"Yeah, but you don't understand. Zach has, like, a genius-level IQ. He's also the most amazing surfer ever! What makes him so incredible is that he has a brain *and* a body. He and Amelia are both incredibly smart."

Amelia felt all warm and happy that Courtney had called her (and Zach) smart. One of the most important things about Amelia's relationship with Courtney was that Courtney really understood Amelia. Courtney really *got* her. There weren't too many people in the world Amelia could say that about. Especially not her brother.

Peekaboo was wagging her tail even more frenetically now. Amelia made eye contact with the dog, which was a big mistake, because she gave a short, sharp yelp.

"Did you hear that bark?" asked Courtney.

"Is that Peekaboo?" asked Piper.

"Where *is* she?" Courtney asked. "I've been looking for her all morning."

Amelia had sort of confiscated Peekaboo about an hour ago, when the dog followed her into the kitchen. (Amelia had wanted a cassis juice, and decided to help herself.)

"So obviously you're totally in love with Zach," Piper said.

No response.

Amelia pressed her ear even closer to the wall, but there was nothing to hear.

She raised her index finger to her pursed lips, a sign for Peekaboo to remain very quiet. She scanned the room, in search of a glass or something that she could put up to the wall to amplify the sound. (She wasn't sure that the trick would really work, or what the scientific basis for it was, but she had seen it on TV tons of times.)

She went over to the dressing table (oh, what she wouldn't do to actually have a dressing table in her life!), which had these amazing ball-and-claw feet, and grabbed the crystal water glass sitting on top. The glass itself was enormously heavy, and had a delicate little bee pattern on it. Amelia went back to the wall and put the glass up against it and her ear up against the open end of the glass. She hoped that she was listening to the right side of the glass, although she couldn't be sure.

The glass sounded like a seashell when your ear was up against it, and the only thing Amelia could hear were the sounds of the ocean. She turned the glass around.

"What does he look like?" Piper asked.

"He looks like . . . he looks like . . . well, I've never seen anyone who looks like him be—"

"Do you have a picture of him?"

"I never took a picture of him in St. Bart's; I was too embarrassed. I guess he looks the most like Johnny Depp. I keep thinking of the word *Cherokee* when I think of him."

Zach had been the recipient of their mother's dark and brooding good looks. Amelia, while she had inherited their mother's deep brown hair, had her father's fair skin and light blue eyes. Amelia had always been a bit envious of Zach's complexion.

"And what about Amelia?" Piper asked. "Do you have a picture of *her*?"

"I do! Do you want to see? On my cell phone."

Amelia's heart sank. What a nightmare—to be stuck secretly listening to two girls (one nice, one not nice) scrutinize your appearance! If Piper said anything mean about her, Amelia would . . . she would . . . well, she wasn't sure what she would do, actually. Probably burst into tears.

"She's *okaaaaay*," Piper said.

What did that mean? "She's *okaaaaay*"? That Amelia wasn't *completely* disgusting, but she wasn't anything to write home about, either?

Come on, Courtney, Amelia thought. *Please defend me! Come on! Show me how much you love me.*

"Well, *I* think Amelia Warner is the most beautiful girl I've ever seen in my whole life," Courtney said.

Yay, Courtney! She was such a good, honorable, loyal friend. Amelia wished there were more like her in the world.

Amelia gave a thumbs-up sign to Peekaboo. The dog assumed a play pose—her bottom in the air and her head down—and wagged her tail like crazy.

"She has nice *hair*," Piper said.

Troll. It was like saying, "Well, she has nice *hair*, but everything else about her is a hot tranny mess."

"You'll meet her soon," Courtney said. "Everything she says is just so *interesting*."

"Interesting people are my favorite kinds of people," Piper said. "Especially people who tell such interesting stories about themselves. What are we waiting for? Is she, like, asleep, or something?"

"I thought I heard her in the guest room a little while ago," Courtney said. "But let's go hang in my room for a few minutes, just in case. Then we can come back and see what she's up to. She's probably reading."

Amelia wasn't going to give Piper the satisfaction of meeting her on her own terms. (Amelia could tell already that Piper was one of those monumentally selfish people who only did things on their own terms.)

She set down her glass and picked up Peekaboo from the bed, giving her a tight hug. She was thinking about how Peekaboo smelled like Acqua di Parma perfume when she noticed a wet spot on the gold bedspread.

Oops. Maybe Peekaboo *wasn't* allowed on the bed.

The Moores had a maid who would take care of that, didn't they? The great thing about the rich was that they hired people to clean up their messes, and the messes other people made.

Amelia put the dog down on the floor and checked

her makeup in the mirror. No mascara issues, so that was good news. She applied her Chanel beige lipstick, gave her hair a few strokes with her Fekkai brush that some right-out-of Harvard hedge-fund manager guy had given her as one of her presents for deigning to give him the pleasure of her company for three dinners, and opened the door. Peekaboo slipped out into the hallway.

Although Amelia knew she wouldn't like Piper Hansen, she was prepared to meet her. Amelia considered herself heroic for taking this step, because heroes often had to do things they didn't want to do. That, in fact, was one definition of a hero, as Amelia's father, the untenured classics professor, would surely point out.

14

The Kindness of Strangers

FRIDAY MORNING, NEW YORK

Courtney and Piper were resettling themselves in Courtney's room. Every summer Friday at this time of day, when they were both in town, Piper would pick up Courtney at her place and they would go get a manicure-pedicure at a place around the block, then have a late lunch and go shopping.

Usually they went to Barneys and had lunch at Fred's, the restaurant on the top floor of the store, which was always packed with people, although the maître d' knew Courtney and Piper and would let them in right away without a wait. Sometimes they went to Bergdorf Goodman, and sometimes, if time was tight, and if

Courtney still felt guilty about spending so much of her parents' money from the week before, they would just go to Sephora.

Courtney looked forward to these Fridays, and she enjoyed them, but in another way she felt guilty about wasting her time and money on such frivolity. Piper, however, didn't seem to share any of Courtney's conflicted feelings about the day; she was a fearless spender of her father's money, and seemed to believe that the goal of her Friday afternoons with Courtney was to spend as much money and to buy as much stuff as possible.

Courtney again considered the picture of Amelia on her cell phone. Amelia really was so pretty. Courtney flipped the phone shut and chucked it into her Chloé Paddington bag, which was lying open on her gilt-framed bed.

Piper was lounging on the dusky rose velvet couch, texting someone (Geoff?).

"I have an idea," Piper said, typing away with swift thumbs, not bothering to look up from her phone. "Why don't you invite their *parents* to live here too? You might as well put up the whole Warner family while you're at it. I'm sure your charity would mean a lot to them."

Courtney didn't feel that it was fair that Piper had such suspicions about her new friends. She didn't appreciate it.

Before she could respond, there was a knock on the door.

Piper looked up from her phone. "Nubby?" she asked flatly.

Piper seemed to think that was the funniest nickname ever, but really it was just bitchy. "No, *Nabby's* not here yet," Courtney said.

She turned the crystal knob. Before her stood her dear new friend Amelia Warner.

Over on the couch, Piper's eyes narrowed and her lips pursed.

"Amelia!" Courtney exclaimed, as if she hadn't seen Amelia for decades.

They did a dual cheek kiss, like two old socialites meeting up at La Goulue.

"I just talked to Zach," Amelia said, her gaze locked on Piper's lounging figure. "And I have good news!"

"Oh my God, what?" Courtney asked.

Was Zach coming back from Paris early? That would definitely be good news. And if he had told Amelia that he was in love, deeply, profoundly in love, with Courtney, that would be even better.

"Aren't you going to introduce us?" Piper asked. Her face was set in a stark smile.

Amelia walked over to the couch and extended her hand to Piper. Piper sort of half-sat and shook Amelia's hand weakly, as if she were a feeble old woman on her deathbed.

"Charmed," Piper said, and then lay back down.

It was so rude and embarrassing that Piper couldn't be bothered to get up, because you were always supposed to stand when you were introduced to someone (this was one of the first things Courtney's mother taught her; she was always polite, even when she had been sunbathing topless on their roof downtown).

"I've heard *so* much about you, Pepper," Amelia said. "It really is a pleasure to meet you."

"Piper," Piper said sweetly. "And the honor is all mine."

"Of course, Piper. Isn't that what I said?"

Courtney stifled a laugh.

"So. Do tell us the good news about Zach," Piper said. "I know I'm just dying to hear."

If Amelia picked up on Piper's sarcasm, she wasn't showing it, which Courtney found gracious and admirable.

"Zach is coming back from Paris tonight! He needed to wrap up his business with Sarkozy early, because Daddy wants him to look at some property in Connecticut. Daddy has been thinking of buying an estate out there for ages, and he's decided that now is the time."

Oh my God. It was too good to be true! Zach was coming home early, and Courtney would get to see him soon. Maybe even tonight!

Piper sat upright. "*Where* in Connecticut?" she asked.

Amelia sat down on the couch, right next to Piper. One of the things that Courtney liked so much about Amelia was her fearlessness. She wasn't shy at all—which Courtney so obviously, and so embarrassingly, was. Piper gave her a sideways glance, as if Amelia were intruding on her space. Amelia didn't seem to notice.

"I don't know the name of the road," Amelia said. "I leave those details to Zach and Daddy."

How cute was it to think about Zach knowing the names of roads, and being able to read maps, and looking at property for their father?

"Where is Zach staying tonight?" Courtney asked. Did she sound way too eager? And would Piper tell Geoff—whom Courtney had almost temporarily forgotten about—that she sounded like an excitable little puppy whenever Zach was the topic of conversation?

It was funny how Courtney's feelings about Geoff had done a complete reversal since she'd met Zach. She wasn't proud of herself for developing such trembling, wild feelings for Zach when she'd thought she'd been in love with Geoff. But it wasn't as if she and Geoff were ever officially dating! Even though she had desperately wished they were. Often, after she saw Geoff, she would come home and cry herself to sleep; it just seemed so *hopeless* with him. *It's just a crush,* she would tell herself, trying to convince herself that a crush had nothing to do with real love. *It's just a crush, and crushes are meaningless; they're meaningless, meaningless.*

"See, *that's* what I wanted to talk to you about," Amelia said. "Our apartment is *such* a mess with the construction, and—"

"Oh, let me guess," Piper said. "You're going to suggest that your brother stay here at the palatial Moore home! What play is that, Courtney, that has the line about the kindness of strangers?"

Courtney wasn't bold—or stupid—enough to tell Piper to pipe down and stop being so aggressive with Amelia. The thing about Piper—and a person would understand this about her only if they'd known her for years—was that she was a very possessive friend. Her behavior toward other people—and Courtney had seen this before, at benefits they'd been to together—seemed, on the surface, very rude, but really, Piper was just letting her insecurity get the better of her.

Courtney's father had made the comment that he believed that Piper liked Courtney so much that she sometimes lashed out whenever she sensed that someone might take Courtney away from her. This had given Courtney some insight into Piper's perspective. Although Piper's perspective still seemed crazy! Like, why couldn't Courtney have more than one friend—two, including Geoff?

"It's *A Streetcar Named Desire*," said Amelia.

Courtney loved that Amelia knew her literary references, and also that she could stand up to Piper. Sometimes Piper really needed someone to put her in her place.

"And, actually," Amelia continued, "Zach and I look forward to repaying Courtney for all of her kindness someday, when our apartment is finished. She'll be welcome to stay whenever she wants."

Hey, that sounded pretty good to Courtney.

"You don't have to repay me," Courtney said, shooting a withering look at Piper.

"Anyway," Amelia said, "I wanted to ask you if it would be possible if Zach could stay here for a day or two. You can imagine how much I hate to ask—"

"I can only imagine," Piper said. She dug into her Fendi baguette (much more appropriate for *evening*, in Courtney's opinion) and produced a tin. "Altoid?" she asked, the Altoids tin flat in her palm. Not to be mean, but Piper really did need a manicure. (She was wearing Repetto ballet flats, so Courtney couldn't see the condition of her feet.) Piper had been going for the old standby Chanel Vamp for the last several weeks ("a classic," she proclaimed) and always brought her own bottle, of course, deeming the salon brands (which Courtney used) inferior.

"No, thank you," Courtney said of the Altoid. She

had always felt that it seemed a little bit rude to take candy and things from people when they were offered.

"Yes, please," Amelia said, and popped an Altoid into her mouth. She crunched very loudly—the sign of an impatient person. Courtney liked that. She wasn't one of those people herself, but she was drawn to people who were in a hurry.

"Zach can stay in the Koi Room," Courtney said. "Do you think he'll like it? Do you think the water trickling in the pond will bother him at night?"

"Isn't it operated on a motor?" Piper asked, tossing two more mints into her mouth. "He can just turn it off."

"I was going to suggest the same thing," Amelia said, helping herself, without asking, to another mint.

"Great minds think alike," Piper said.

"I was just going to say the same thing," Amelia said. Then there were a few vigorous crunches.

This whole meeting between Amelia and Piper seemed to have really turned a corner. It seemed to be going better than Courtney had predicted. And now with Zach staying in the Koi Room tonight . . .

"Well, I guess we should go soon and beautify for our special visitor," Piper said.

Which brought to mind the superficial, yet still important question: What was Courtney going to wear tonight for Zach?

Tonight for Zach: those modest three words made her practically shiver.

Amelia stood. Piper gave her the old once-over with her eyes.

"Do you want to come with, Amelia?" Piper asked. "We're off to get a mani-pedi."

Piper had committed two of Courtney's biggest pet peeves in the space of only two sentences. *Come with* had always irritated Courtney, as did *mani-pedi*.

Anyway, Courtney was glad that Piper had invited Amelia, but she hoped that the invitation didn't seem too belated. She didn't want Amelia to think that she and Piper were planning some kind of activity without including her.

"I'd adore it," Amelia said. "I have my bottle of Chanel Vamp in my bag."

"Too bizarre," Courtney said. "That's Piper's color too."

Piper stood and faced Amelia defiantly, like an empress outraged at her reflection.

"I knew you two would get along," said Courtney, even though she hadn't known that at all, despite how many times she'd tried to convince Piper (and herself) of the possibility.

This afternoon, after their manicure-pedicures, Courtney could definitely buy something to wear at

Barneys or Bergdorf Goodman for tonight. But then again, she had this periwinkle Alberta Ferretti dress her mother had bought her before they went to St. Bart's. Courtney wasn't sure that she liked it, though—it was cut on a bias, and its main design element was these wacky cutout circles. She couldn't decide if the dress was cool or weird. Courtney was leaning toward the latter, but she needed Piper and Amelia to either second (and third) her opinion, or else refute it.

Amelia and Piper were still standing, facing each other and staring like two dangerous animals.

"Do you guys think you could give me an opinion on a dress?"

"Delighted to," both Piper and Amelia said simultaneously. It was like hearing something in surround sound.

Courtney padded across her silk Persian rug (her father, who didn't like her to take anything for granted, often reminded her that the rug was bigger than most people's apartments in New York, including the one in the East Village where they had lived when Courtney was born). She opened the door to her closet and stepped inside. Her closet was one of her favorite places in the whole apartment—and not only because it housed hundreds of thousands of dollars' worth of haute couture (and also some diffusion lines). She liked it mostly because it was so spectacularly well organized, and as systematic as the library at Hawthorne.

The closet cleared her head whenever she stepped into it. It was arranged alphabetically, according to the names of the designers, but then in subsets according to season, and then occasion type. There were two full-length mirrors, a dressing table with a three-angled mirror, a settee, and another velvet couch.

Courtney went right to the front of the closet to the Alberta Ferretti section (the Alexander McQueen section came right after), then to the blue/purple area, then to the casual-evening-wear section of that. She pulled out the dress, which still had the Bergdorf's tag on it. Should she try it on so Amelia and Piper could have a better sense of what the dress *really* looked like?

She decided to bring the dress out on its padded hanger. When she reemerged into her bedroom, she saw Amelia and Piper standing in profile, facing each other, both with their hands set on their hips. There was something about Amelia and Piper that seemed similar. It wasn't so much that they looked alike as it was that there was something akin about their characters. Maybe Amelia was a more refined, more enlightened version of Piper? Something like that.

Courtney held the dress up.

"What do you think?" she asked.

"Hate it," Piper said.

"Detest it," Amelia said. "Looks like someone's craft project in day camp."

"I was going to say the exact same thing," Piper said. "I was going to use that exact word: 'crafty.'"

God, was the dress really *that* bad? Courtney considered it again. It must have been, if Amelia and Piper both held precisely the same stern opinion. Although Piper did often get on her nerves, Courtney relied on her advice more than she did on anyone else's.

Except, maybe, now Amelia's.

15

Four Is a Crowd; Five Is Better

FRIDAY NIGHT, NEW YORK

Courtney, Amelia, Piper, and Geoff were seated at a table at the Bemelmans Bar at the Carlyle Hotel. The venue was Courtney's suggestion, because it was one of her favorite places in the whole world, next to her closet. It was such a refined, classy place—a clubby, immaculate little jewel box of a room, with low gold ceilings and high tufted leather banquettes. Watercolor murals, the color of ice cream and confetti, depicting anthropomorphized animals, wrapped the perimeter of the room. They were painted by Ludwig Bemelmans, the author and illustrator of the *Madeline* books, which were some of Courtney's favorite books ever.

And Courtney adored the Carlyle Hotel too. It was filled with so many pleasant memories for Courtney, because she and her mother had spent many nights here years ago when their apartment was being renovated. The Carlyle and the Pierre—and maybe, to a lesser extent, the St. Regis—were the most luxurious (read: most expensive) hotels in New York. The Carlyle was the coolest, though, because it was all art deco and Hollywood thirties glam. If the Carlyle were filmed, it would be shot in evocative black-and-white.

Everyone—except for Amelia—was making fun of Courtney for her suggestion of Bemelmans.

"I always said Courtney was a true octogenarian at heart," Piper said as she took a sip of her champagne cocktail.

Courtney had no idea what was in a champagne cocktail, but she liked that it seemed so intimidatingly adult. So did Geoff's drink of choice—a Stinger. What the hell was that?

Here was one of the other many great things about Amelia, though: just when Piper and Geoff were getting sort of cool, yet mostly superpretentious cocktails, Amelia had ordered a beer. Granted, it was an eighteen-dollar Chimay, but it was a beer all the same.

"Well, I think the major thing about this bar is that we

didn't get carded," said Geoff.

"Geoff, haven't you learned yet?" asked Piper. "The major thing about really prestigious bars for elderly people like this one is that they would never think to card you. They're too polite. Besides, the bartenders have probably never met anyone under forty here, so they just forgot what young people look like."

"I've noticed this phenomenon too," Amelia said as she fiddled with the base of her beer glass. (All of the better places, Courtney had noticed, served beer in glasses with stems.) "The bar with the chicest glasses of all time has to be Harry's Bar in Rome."

"Love it there," Piper said. "We always stay at a hotel right across the street from Harry's, and Daddy always makes us go there for a nightcap."

"My father adores Harry's Bar in Venice," said Amelia.

Here was another thing they had in common! There were so many things they had in common, it was turning out. When all three girls got their manicures-pedicures this afternoon, Amelia and Piper were just chatting away about places they'd been, and celebrities they knew, and shows they'd seen, and stores they liked—and it had turned out that they'd been to all the same places, knew all the same celebrities, seen all the same shows, and shopped at all the same stores.

Anyway, Amelia seemed to be getting along so well

with Piper and Geoff. Especially with Geoff.

Geoff was sitting really close to Amelia, and their hands were almost touching on the top of the table. Courtney had noticed that Geoff had been asking Amelia lots of questions, and holding doors open for her, and laughing really loudly at her jokes. Courtney was ninety percent happy that Geoff seemed to like Amelia so much, but that meant that ten percent of her wasn't really happy.

Okay, she was *eighty* percent happy and *twenty* percent unhappy.

The confusing thing was that Geoff did look pretty cute tonight. Courtney had to give him credit for that. He was wearing beige linen pants and a beautifully pressed Thomas Pink shirt, and he was glisteningly tan.

"How many times have you been to Venice?" asked Piper.

"Tons," Amelia said. "Probably about twenty times. I *love* St. Mark's Square. It's easily one of the most beautiful places in the universe."

"I totally agree," Geoff said. "I love standing in the square and having the pigeons land on your arm."

God, everything that Amelia said, Geoff would respond to by going, "I couldn't agree more!" Was Courtney maybe even a little bit jealous? Right now, in anticipation of Zach's arrival, she knew she shouldn't be thinking about Geoff at all. But it was so hard not to.

Having a crush on him had become second nature.

"Gross," Piper said. "Birds are gross. They freak me out."

Courtney knew about Piper's bird phobia. One day earlier in the summer, when they were out walking Courtney's dog in Central Park, Piper seemed to think that a pigeon, who was innocently flapping its wings high above their heads, was going to dive-bomb right into her face. She screamed and dropped to the ground, totally ruining her Wolford tights.

Courtney took a drink of her Shirley Temple. Yes, she knew how dorked-out it was to order a Shirley Temple, but this time she ordered it spiked with rum. She could barely taste the alcohol and she wondered if the bartender had forgotten it. But it was so delicious the way the sweet grenadine cut the acidity of the orange juice, and then, of course, the big treat at the end: a cherry. She couldn't really tell yet, because she had consumed maybe only about a third of her drink, but it looked as if there could possibly be three cherries in the bottom of her glass, which was two cherries more than most places gave you.

Amelia was looking over at Courtney in a sweet way. She smiled.

"Can I tell you how much I love that new dress?" Amelia asked.

Courtney had bought the dress in the Chanel salon

at Bergdorf Goodman. It was a layered, flapper-inspired number with a low-slung waist. Thank God Amelia and Piper had saved her from the Alberta Ferretti train wreck. That was the last time Courtney let her mother pick out a dress for her.

Courtney patted the flower in her hair. "But can I tell you how the gardenia makes the whole look?"

"The flower in the hair *is* genius," Piper said. Get a couple of champagne cocktails into Piper, and she could turn as kind and as generous as Mother Teresa.

Amelia had basically acted as Courtney's stylist for tonight. It was Amelia's sole idea to stop into Takashimaya, the cool Japanese department store on Fifth Avenue, after they had finished at Bergdorf Goodman, and buy a flower to put in Courtney's hair. Amelia chose the most perfect, most pristine single gardenia that the earth had ever produced.

When they got home, Amelia styled Courtney's hair in a complex yet simple updo, which involved about five hundred bobby pins. Then, as the pièce de résistance, Amelia slid the gardenia into Courtney's hair, on the side.

Courtney felt like a heroine in an F. Scott Fitzgerald novel tonight. She hoped that Zach liked the style, which was, Courtney had to admit, kind of out there. None of the girls at Hawthorne were really rocking the late-twenties vibe.

"Zach is going to be blown away when he sees you

tonight," Amelia said, as if she were reading Courtney's mind.

A quizzical look flashed across Geoff's face.

"Who is *Zach* again?" he asked.

It seemed weird to Courtney that Geoff didn't know who Zach was, because they had—or at least Courtney had—talked about him quite extensively during the last few days. She vividly remembered the first time she brought Zach up to Geoff: it had been when they were at the charity ball. Oh my God—were Amelia's and Geoff's legs touching? Courtney couldn't tell what was going on underneath the tablecloth, but she hoped not. Wait, no, she didn't care. The exquisite torture of conflicting crushes!

"Zach is Amelia's twin brother," Piper said, "and he's coming back from Paris tonight."

"Oh yeahhhhh," Geoff said. "That sounds familiar. I remember hearing something about that. I'll have to try out my French with him. It'll be good to know someone else who's fluent."

Geoff had been brought up in a bilingual household, and he had actually spoken French before he'd learned to speak English. Their nanny was a French girl . . . who unfortunately had an affair for years—like, until Geoff was twelve—with Geoff's father, thereby causing Geoff's parents to get a divorce. Geoff had supposedly never really spoken French, except in school, since then.

"Well, see, here's the thing," Amelia said. "Zach gets *really* self-conscious about speaking French in the States. His accent is so natural that it makes him feel like an asshole when he speaks it to nonnatives."

Courtney went all warm and tingly again. Zach was just so brilliant and modest and sweet, and was so conscious of other people's feelings that he didn't want to make anyone feel bad about their comparatively poor French-speaking ability.

She was so excited to see him tonight . . . she was so, so excited that she almost couldn't stand it.

"And what was he doing in Paris again?" Piper asked.

"He was doing some work for President Sarkozy," Amelia said.

"*How* old are you guys again?" asked Piper.

"Eighteen," Amelia said. Courtney tried to make a mental note, because she kept getting their age confused. She had thought Amelia said seventeen earlier.

"And he's accomplished this much already in his life?" Geoff asked. "While I've just spent the summer so far on Daddy's boat in East Hampton? Pardon me while I go and shoot myself in the head now."

To be fair, Geoff did have this winning side to him. Like, even though he *seemed* pompous sometimes, he was actually totally vulnerable. Now Courtney was feeling slightly, just slightly, squishy for him all over again. Could someone have a crush on two guys simultaneously? Was her heart big enough for that?

Although Zach *was* definitely more accomplished than Geoff could ever hope to be . . .

"I wouldn't worry about that, Geoff," Piper said teasingly. "Nobody expects you to accomplish all that much anyway."

"Gee, thanks," replied Geoff.

Amelia's cell phone rang on the table.

"Zachary!" she shrieked into the phone. "How was the flight?"

Piper and Geoff exchanged glances.

"Say that again? Who was on the flight from Paris? Vanessa Paradis was in first class across the aisle from you?"

The idea that Zach was on the phone, in New York, made Courtney's heart race. And just like that she'd forgotten all about Geoff's vulnerable side again.

In the mural over the bar two rabbits rowed a canoe, and another rabbit aimed a rifle into the sky. Courtney was considering how the pictures she liked best were the ones for children, as she continued eavesdropping on Amelia's conversation with her devastatingly hot brother.

"Really?" Amelia was saying. "Well, if you're feeling that wrecked maybe you should just have the car take you straight home."

Oh no. No, no, no. Courtney felt herself starting to deflate, but suddenly she was seized by a weird feeling. What was it? Bravery? Boldness? Stupidity? Had the bartender spiked her Shirley Temple with *two* shots of rum?

"Tell him to come over and hang with us," Courtney said. "At least for a little while."

Piper raised her eyebrows at her as if to say, *What has gotten into you, Courtney Moore?*

Courtney pretended not to notice. Geoff blinked rapidly and moved his hand even closer to Amelia's.

"I have a request," Amelia said into the phone. "A very special someone has asked for you to come by. . . . Well, it *is* better to stay awake after a flight, adjust to the time zone and all. . . . Great! We're at Bemelmans Bar. Do you know where that is?" Amelia paused and furrowed her brow. "Where is it again?" she asked the table.

"I thought you said you practically *lived* at the Carlyle when you were a kid," said Piper.

Amelia narrowed her eyes at Piper.

"East Seventy-sixth Street," said Geoff.

"It's at East Seventy-sixth Street," Amelia repeated, "and Madison Avenue."

Oh my God, oh my God. Courtney was going to hyperventilate. *I must remain calm; I must remain calm,* she told herself. In her head she went over her speech to Zach. *I know that your apartment is being renovated—I've lived through that hellaciousness too!—so I think it would be a great idea if you stayed at our place for a few days.*

In my bed, Courtney thought.

She couldn't believe how hot and bothered she got whenever she thought about Zach. Geoff had never made her feel that way—never, ever. He was just too G-rated. Or at least their relationship was.

Maybe that was it: her love for Geoff was totally platonic. Like a brother (or maybe a distant cousin?)—and she had only just realized that.

"Okay, then, see you soon!" said Amelia, and the phone call with Courtney's future husband reached its conclusion.

"Where's he going to store his bags?" asked Piper. "The bar is too crowded for luggage."

"Oh, he travels light. But he knows all of the doormen," Amelia said, "so I'm sure they'll keep the bags for him if he needs them to."

"Why don't *you* seem to know the doormen?" asked Piper.

"I know them," Amelia said, shutting the proverbial door on that question.

Amelia and Piper were already verbally sparring as if they were sisters. Courtney wished she could take it as an encouraging sign that they felt so comfortable together but . . . she was an optimist not an idiot.

16

A Case of Mistaken Identity?

FRIDAY NIGHT, NEW YORK

The bus ride from Concord, New Hampshire, wasn't so bad, because Zach slept for most of it. Usually he had a hard time getting any shut-eye on buses, but not today. When he woke up, they were pulling into the Port Authority bus terminal.

Zach had learned to pack lightly during all his years of traveling with his sister, who always demanded that he carry her bags for her—and Amelia brought a *lot* of bags on her trips. He had only one small duffel with him, although the thought did occur to him that he would certainly have more bags if he'd just flown in from Paris. He'd considered bringing a bigger bag to make his Paris trip more believable, then decided against it when he realized that was a little too deceitful for him. Whenever he felt himself doing something Amelia would do, or even considering it, it freaked him out. It was one thing to go along with Amelia's lies; it was another to actively support them.

Sometimes Amelia's lies—like this one about Zach being President Sarkozy's intern (who was she kidding?)—were totally out of left field and made zero sense. He'd have to figure out a way to play this one down. Amelia's problem, one of them, was that there was no filter between her brain and her mouth. Other times it seemed as if she actually said things *before* she thought them.

He made his way through the crush of lumpen, ugly people at Port Authority. Zach considered getting a smoothie, but thought better of it. Although he was hungry, he needed to save his money, and the smoothies at Smoothie King would set him back seven bucks.

Zach took the subway uptown, something Amelia would never approve of, because she would never rub shoulders with "those types of people," as she said. His pampered sister preferred cabs, and, more accurately, town cars, charged to the accounts of guys Zach had never heard of before.

It was beginning to get on Zach's nerves how he—how *they* (his father, his sister, himself)—never had any money. Since they'd been back from St. Bart's, he'd earned only about a hundred and twenty bucks at his job. That was all the cash Zach had in his shorts pocket, and it had to last the whole weekend in New York. If he were on his own, he could easily spread the money out—he'd take the subway or walk wherever he needed to go; he would get a deli bagel in the morning, some hard-boiled eggs for lunch, and two hot dogs from Gray's Papaya for dinner.

But Amelia was so expensive in her tastes (as long as someone else was paying for her, which someone else always was, although rarely did anyone else ever pay for Zach) that it cost a fortune just to be around her. The sad thing was that Zach couldn't keep up with his sister's lifestyle . . . and *he* was the one with the *job*! Amelia was right about one thing: life was unfair most of the time.

Zach felt kind of like a bum as he walked into the Carlyle Hotel lobby. Everyone else there was about seventy, and dressed as if they were going to the Kentucky Derby. The doormen shot him dirty looks, and one old dude, who was wearing, literally, white gloves, asked him if he was a guest of the hotel. He thought for a second that he was going to get thrown out because of his beat-up old shorts from junior high.

Zach just smiled at the old guy and admitted that he wasn't a hotel guest; then he asked where the bar was. He supposed that Amelia had chosen this bar because it was superexpensive, and also because they didn't card.

Into the bar he walked, with his duffel bag slung over his shoulder. On the wall were paintings of animals in clothes, doing stuff that humans did, like rowing boats in ponds. In the middle distance a hand was waving at him. That hand belonged to his sister, Ann. Amelia. *Whatevs.* He just had to remember not to call her Ann tonight, in front of her new friends. She would destroy him if he slipped and called her by her real name.

He walked toward the table. Amelia was there with Courtney, naturally, and with two other kids. He couldn't see who they were yet.

"Brother of mine! I'm sooooo happy to see you!" Amelia squealed, and threw her arms around Zach's neck.

She had probably never hugged him with such enthusiasm, which concerned him, and made him wonder if it was all for show. Amelia smelled as if she had bathed in perfume. Every centimeter of her face was covered with thick makeup, and she was wearing more jewelry than Zach had ever seen on any one person. Were those *real* diamond earrings? Of course they were, knowing Amelia. (And what guy—or girl—had she charmed, then abandoned, to get those earrings?) She looked older, and maybe not in a good way.

Courtney stood up, and she and Zach looked at each

other. She was obviously blushing, and she averted her eyes. Zach lunged in to give her a little peck on the cheek. Courtney was such a nice girl—a "good egg," as Zach's father liked to call nice people—and he hoped that Amelia didn't mess with her too much. Zach would kill Amelia if she hurt Courtney, as she'd done with so many others.

"Hey, Courtney," he said. "You look nice."

Courtney blushed some more and patted at a white flower in her hair. She looked sophisticated and pretty, but what had possessed her to put that flower in her hair? The flower was slightly, just slightly, lame.

Zach thought he recognized the others from the pictures that Amelia made him look at that afternoon in St. Bart's. The girl—what was her name? Amelia had said it about a million times—looked like a young Uma Thurman, and the guy looked like a tool. A pastel-colored sweater was knotted around his neck. Did it get any more toolish than that?

The girl (Pepper? No, that couldn't be right) was attractive, but she had really angular features, and there was something a little bit too harsh and pinched about her face and body. Courtney was prettier. The guy (Geoff with a G, no doubt) was blond and pale, and looked like a male model in a Ralph Lauren ad. He was probably about as bright as a model in a Ralph Lauren ad too.

"Aren't you going to introduce us?" asked the girl.

She extended her right hand in the air and dropped her fingertips. Did she expect Zach to, like, kiss her hand or something?

Without really thinking too much about it, Zach bent down and planted a debonair kiss on her hand.

"You must have learned that in France," she said, giggling, which didn't seem like something that came naturally to her.

"*Oui, oui,*" Zach said, smiling.

As soon as he said that, he wished that he hadn't, because then everyone would think he spoke French. Also, it made him feel really stupid.

Courtney scooted back into her seat.

"Zach," Amelia said, "I'd like you to meet my new friends Piper and Geoff."

Piper. Right. Both Piper and Geoff with a G grinned at Zach. Zach grinned back and sat down next to Courtney.

An elderly waiter in a short red jacket approached the table and asked Zach for his order. Zach glanced around the table and determined that everyone was drinking alcohol. And was squeaky-clean Courtney drinking a real cocktail too? What kind of drink was that red-orange color and had a cherry? A whiskey sour?

"I'll have a double Jack Daniel's," Zach said.

Then Zach privately freaked out, because he didn't

know how he was going to pay for it. A double Jack would probably cost about twenty bucks, which would leave only a hundred for the whole weekend. He had to learn to conserve his money better.

"Very good, sir," said the waiter.

"That sounds delish," Piper said. "Give me one of those, too."

"Indeed," said the waiter.

Piper was pretty hot, now that Zach was getting a better look at her. There was something really attractive, although in a dangerous way, about her. It was like she could rip you into pieces in a second . . . but, despite the pain, and despite the fact that you would soon be dead, you would enjoy the experience of letting Piper have her sick way with you.

Geoff leaned forward and put his elbows on the table, as if he were going to say something.

"*Comment êtes-vous ce soir?*" Geoff asked. "*Comment a été votre vol?*"

Damn. Zach *knew* that the whole France lie that his so-called brilliant sister had concocted would come back to bite him in the ass. He shouldn't have said that "*oui, oui*" thing. *Idiot.*

"Don't you mean '*Comment* allez-*vous*'?" Piper asked.

Before Zach could even register what was happening (and note that he wouldn't have to feel threatened by Geoff's superior French skills but that he might want to be careful around Piper), Amelia came in for the save.

"Oh, your flight was great, wasn't it?" she asked. Amelia didn't speak French either. How did she know what Geoff had said? "You remember what I told you about Zach being all self-conscious about speaking in French. Zach, you sat next to Vanessa Paradis in first class, didn't you?"

"Uh, yeahhhh," he replied.

This scam was getting too stupid, and too involved. *Did I ask to be dragged into this vortex of lies?* Zach wondered. He often asked the same question whenever Amelia—*Ann, her frickin' name is Ann; can we please send out a press release?*—created a whole new identity for him, one that he had nothing to do with, and one that he had no choice but to go along with. Like the lie that he was Johnny Depp's brother. That was one that Amelia had once told some movie producer wunderkind, in the hope that . . . what? What had she even hoped to accomplish by that lie? Her brief involvement with the movie producer, who wasn't even twenty-one, did yield a diamond bracelet that she had been very psyched about at the time, and a couple cashmere sweaters.

Whatever his sister's relationship with someone, there was always something she wanted to get in return.

His drink came, thank God, and Zach pounded it.

"That's so cool, though, to get to work for the president of France," Piper said. She was slurring her words just a little bit. She seemed slightly drunk, which was good, because it meant that she wouldn't dig too deeply into this I-worked-for-Sarkozy BS.

"Yeah." Zach decided to try to do some damage control. "I'm not really working for Sarkozy." Amelia shot him a look. "I was just interviewing with one of his advisers. Amelia, you have to stop exaggerating my accomplishments." He smiled at his sister and she smiled back. He was sure that no one at the table knew what the smiles were really conveying.

His: *Stop telling such ridiculous stories about me.* (Also: *Please don't kill me.*)

Hers: *I'm going to kill you, you little shit.*

There was a grand piano in the room, and the man seated at it was playing old Frank Sinatra songs. Geoff put his arm around Courtney and swayed to the music. He seemed drunk too.

Zach watched Courtney delicately remove Geoff's arm, and then felt her move closer to him. *Sucks for you, Geoff with a G.*

"I just wanted . . . to tell you," Courtney said in a whisper. Was she almost stuttering? "You're welcome to stay in our apartment while yours is being renovated."

She hadn't even been able to make eye contact as she whispered her invitation. But Zach thought that he had *already* been invited to stay at Courtney's apartment, and that the matter had been dealt with.

Also, what was the thing about renovating their father's apartment? If that had been a lie Amelia had concocted, he couldn't remember it. He supposed that she had made up some shit about the work they were having done at their apartment at the Plaza Hotel or something.

Whatever. The double Jack was softening his resolve, and he was ready to just play along. Playing along was really all he was good for in Amelia's world.

Suddenly Amelia's blue eyes widened as she stared at something across the room. She gasped and put her hand over her mouth, then seemed to remember where she was, and, like, willed her face to rearrange itself into an expression of nonchalance. Zach had seen that expression of terror from his sister before, and it never meant good things.

No one else in the group had noticed Amelia's distress. Courtney was staring at her hands, which were folded demurely across the tabletop, and Piper and Geoff were singing along with the Sinatra song.

Zach followed his sister's gaze across the room. Taking a seat at a table in the corner was a couple, a guy and a girl maybe a few years older than they were. He took a closer look at the guy. He looked sort of familiar.

"My darlings," announced Amelia, gathering up her bag, "I've got to run to the loo. Be back in a flash."

"Cool," said Geoff, who was staring directly at Amelia's chest. *Yet another reason to want to deck him,* Zach thought.

"Thanks for the update," said Piper.

"We'll miss you," said Courtney with total sincerity.

Amelia marched through the bar with the seriousness of a soldier. Zach watched as his sister brought her hand up to her face to shield herself from the couple at the table.

But the guy got a look at her, and his face twisted from confused recognition into a mask of insane outrage. He leaped up.

"Ann!" he shouted.

He ran over to Amelia. She stood totally still, as if she were paralyzed.

Zach totally recognized the guy now: he was someone Amelia hung out with last summer and then unceremoniously blew off. The dude went to Princeton, Zach remembered, and Amelia had lost interest in him when she found out he was a scholarship student.

At Zach's table, Courtney, Piper, and Geoff all turned their attention to the scene unfolding in front of them in the middle of the room.

"Does she know that guy? Why did he call her Ann?" asked Piper.

"What did he call her?" asked Geoff sleepily.

"He called her *Ann*," said Piper.

Everyone was looking at him for an answer. Zach wished he could disappear. Defending his absurd sister really was becoming a full-time job.

The guy got up into Amelia's face and started wagging his finger and pointing at her in an insane way, as if he were stabbing her.

"Does she *know* him?" asked Piper again.

"No clue," Zach said.

He was recalling more details about the guy: he had really been into Amelia, and kept calling her and calling her at their house in Massachusetts (they had lived there then, while their father had a job as an adjunct lecturer at a community college).

The girl from the blown-off dude's table went up to Amelia now and started yelling at her too. It seemed as if everyone in the bar were staring.

The girl said to Amelia, "I hope you burn in hell."

Zach saw Amelia's mouth move—she was giving some kind of charming excuse, of course, and watched as she started to walk away from her assailants.

He turned back to the table.

"Case of mistaken identity," he said, and shrugged.

"Happens all the time."

As he said that, he wondered who his sister could be mistaken for. Amelia loved to convince herself that she looked like a younger, thinner Elizabeth Taylor, although Zach had never been able to see the resemblance. He had someone else in mind, someone who seemed much more like his sister: Queen Mary I, perhaps, who was otherwise known as "Bloody Mary," because of all the people she killed.

17

A Girl Walks into a Bar . . .

FRIDAY NIGHT, NEW YORK

"Give me back what you stole from me!"

The dude yelling at Amelia was someone she had hung out with—mercifully briefly—last summer. Amelia was still having a hard time placing his name. Was it Simon? *Let's call him Simon,* she thought. Although he was looking a whole lot less cute now than he was at the beginning of last summer.

Amelia and "Simon" had had this heavy thing for about two months—if that—last summer. He had been a junior at Princeton, and, even though it was summer, he still lived in his dorm at school. The dorm thing should have been a red flag to Amelia immediately, since all of the truly outstanding people always moved off-campus the first semester of their sophomore year, but he was so cute, and they had had so much fun together, and then when he casually mentioned that his ancestors had been Prussian royalty, Amelia became *really* interested. . . .

But old Simon really fell for Amelia, hard and fast. There was no bigger turnoff than when dudes fell for you hard and fast, except maybe when they were broke. Poor old Simon was guilty on both counts. After about three dates Simon started calling Amelia all the time, and texting her, and sending her emails. Frequently he would creepily ask Amelia for her address, which she couldn't give him because: 1. She had lied about where she lived, and had told him that, during the school year, she did "fieldwork in Peru," but that she was recharging her batteries for a few months at her father's estate in Larchmont (she was living with Uncle Mike in his Hell's Kitchen pit last summer, naturally, while her father thought she was taking a summer class at NYU and bunking with one of her boarding school friends), and 2. She got the idea, very quickly, that Simon had a bit of the stalker in him.

The girl with Simon tonight in the Bemelmans Bar was short and chunky, and she seemed to be relishing her role as the Simon sidekick. (*Ick. Why?*) The girl looked pretty familiar, and Amelia decided that she was his sister. Amelia had probably met her once or twice last year, but she always had a hard time remembering uninteresting people. Amelia didn't have a clue about the girl's name; she couldn't even come up with an educated guess.

"Do I know you?" Amelia said, and tried to hide her wrist—her left wrist, her watch wrist—behind her back. She had a half-formed idea that pretending she had never seen Simon before in her life was the way to go.

She glanced back toward her table and saw everyone there—Zach, Courtney, Piper, and Geoff—staring at her with rapt attention. She had to get out of this situation ASAP. She hoped that Zach was able to come up with some excuse to explain the dude's furor. (Mistaken identity? That was always a good one.) If this problem wasn't dealt with and swept away, she could see the whole con with Courtney—and now also with Piper and Geoff—going up in a puff of smoke. She had to be careful and play this well, very, very well.

"Do you still have my *watch*, Ann?" Simon shouted.

"And the bracelet you stole from Sam," brayed the sister.

Oops. Sam, not Simon.

Hey, now, wait a minute. That wasn't fair—neither of those items was stolen. *They were gifts, thank you very much, gifts from my old friend* Sam.

Amelia still had the watch, although she had gotten sick of it and kept it pretty much hidden in her dresser drawer in their pathetic apartment in Vespasian. It was a TAG Heuer watch, which was nice enough to wear if you had to go hiking, or bike riding, or do something otherwise outdoorsy, and maybe you could get away with it for a weekend brunch, when you were wearing a pilled cashmere cardigan, and you did your hair up in a sloppy-chic bun. But that was about it. She hadn't even wanted it; she'd just put it on one night when she saw it on his dresser, and he'd told her it looked hot on her and that she should keep it.

And the bracelet had been a gift too.

Sam was glaring at Amelia so ferociously that she thought he was going to growl at her. Or bite her. Suddenly he grabbed her left arm and wrenched it from behind her back.

"You stupid idiot!" Amelia cried. He was really hurting her, the freak. If he left a bruise, she would *destroy* him, she swore. It wouldn't be pretty. "How *dare* you?" she asked imperiously.

Zach leaped up from the table and rushed over to her. He was followed by Courtney, then Piper, then Geoff.

"Is that the *watch* you gave her?" asked idiot Sam's idiot sister.

Here was a question: why did they seem so concerned about her watch, which had probably cost about seven hundred dollars, when Sam had also given her a diamond-encrusted bracelet that was supposedly some family heirloom (albeit an ugly one)?

Naturally Amelia had sold the bracelet to one of Uncle Mike's sketchy acquaintances. The guy gave her only two grand, though; she knew she was getting ripped off, but she figured that she would rather take a lesser price from Uncle Mike's guy than endure the humiliation of going to a pawnshop in Chinatown. It was embarrassing enough going to this dicey guy's apartment in Queens to pick up an oil-stained envelope with two thousand dollars in it in hundred-dollar bills.

But she'd had a good time that night because Amelia felt flush with money—flush with her *own money*, for the first time in her godforsaken life—and treated herself, Zach, and Uncle Mike to dinner at Del Posto on Tenth Avenue. Dinner cost about three of those hundred-dollar bills, and Amelia, who didn't often take people to dinner, never let Zach or Uncle Mike forget what she had spent on them.

Sam yanked Amelia's wrist, with the Cartier Courtney had bought on it, up to his face. He was stronger than Amelia had remembered, not to mention nastier and uglier. Sam seemed to have gotten taller, but what he'd gained in height he had also gained in body hair. (There was even—*quelle horreur*—hair on his *knuckles*.)

"What is this?!" Sam asked. "*Cartier*? Did you steal

this from some *other* guy?"

"Hardly," Amelia said, feeling proud of herself for being able to tell the truth.

The last time she checked, Courtney Moore was all girl, the most feminine specimen you'd ever meet in your life. Actually, this was something that worried Amelia: Courtney was so much more feminine, so much more girlish than Amelia herself was, and—this was difficult for Amelia to admit to herself—so much prettier.

Zach was on the scene now, and he got right up into Sam's face like an angry baseball coach screaming at an umpire. A semicircle consisting of Courtney, Piper, and Geoff was forming around her. Now that she had settled on a course of action, Amelia was less panicked and instead felt supergrateful that she was surrounded, in both a literal and also a metaphorical sense, by such good friends.

"Take your hands off my sister!" Zach said.

Finally, Sam did unhand Amelia. He stepped back and held his hands up in the air in a gesture of surrender.

"Hey, easy now," he told Zach. *"Eeeeasy."*

Stupid Sam seemed scared that Zach was going to punch him. What a weenie this dude was. She wanted to give him a good smack-down herself.

Sweet Courtney gave Amelia a big hug. Amelia shook her arm, then cradled it against her chest. She decided that if Sam had given her a bruise, she was going to sue.

Geoff asked Amelia if she was okay. She shook her head and wondered if she should start pretending to cry. Would that increase everyone's sympathy, or would a crying jag merely make her seem pitiful? It was a fine line, but Amelia was a subtle artist—a genius at nuance, really—and was always able to balance situations marvelously well.

Piper took a step toward hairy Sam. It seemed disgusting to Amelia that she had dated him. Now *Piper* got all up in his face.

"My mother always said you were a jerk," Piper said, placing an index finger threateningly on his chest.

Wait a minute. A couple of things were worth pointing out here. First of all, *Piper* knew Sam? Secondly, *Piper* was defending Amelia. Funny how things were working out. Although Amelia had a sneaking suspicion that Piper still disliked her, Amelia felt that maybe she was beginning to win her respect. Or maybe Piper was being nice just because she was drunk? Some people turned into angels when they were drunk, although most people turned into ghouls, so maybe Piper was one of the few former.

"Do I *know* you?" asked the sister, giving Piper the once-over.

A bartender in a red bolero jacket approached from one side of the bar, and a doorman in a tuxedo and white gloves approached from the other side. It had taken them long enough, Amelia thought. Although, in all fairness, this wasn't the kind of place that was probably used to bar fights.

"Is there some kind of problem here, folks?" asked the doorman.

"I'm going to have to ask you to leave if there's a problem," said the bartender.

"Don't look at *us*," said Geoff. "This *psycho*"—he gestured to Sam—"attacked this innocent young lady." He nodded at Amelia. Amelia liked that Geoff called her "innocent"; it had been a long time since anyone had described her that way. It almost made her emotional to think back to that innocent time in her life, that time when her mother still existed to them.

After her mother had left without so much as a word, her father wouldn't even allow Amelia and Zach to utter the word *Mommy*. How pitiful was that? How many girls had grown up with a ban on *Mommy*?

It was time to turn on the waterworks. Amelia drew deep into herself and remembered when her mother was still her mother, and when she lived with them, and still combed Amelia's hair at night, and then tucked her into bed. It was hard not to become a cynical person when your own mother left you when you were so young that you still liked it when she tucked you in.

"He hurt me," Amelia wailed. She started bawling torrents of tears.

"I'm going to have to ask you two to leave," the bartender repeated, addressing Sam and his sister.

The looks on their faces as they were escorted out were priceless. Amelia would have laughed if she hadn't already been crying.

18

Oh, What a Night

FRIDAY NIGHT, NEW YORK

Courtney was still buzzing from the excitement at the bar. She had never been part of an altercation—or, okay, an *almost* altercation—before, and she had to admit that it was a little bit exciting.

Courtney had paid the bill, although Amelia kept saying over and over again how she had done so much for them already, and that she should let *Amelia* pay for once. There was *no way* Courtney was going to let Amelia pay for drinks, not after what she'd been through. Courtney had never seen anyone as rude and as hateful as that hairy little guy. The gall of accusing *Amelia* of stealing from him. It was true, what she'd always suspected: some people—most people—were not to be trusted.

Amelia still seemed slightly wobbly and upset as they departed through the Carlyle Hotel lobby. Who could blame her? Courtney probably would have collapsed into a quivering puddle of tears if a strange guy grabbed her in a bar and accused her of being a thief. Courtney couldn't imagine how it felt for Amelia. She slung her arm around her shoulders, which seemed to give Amelia some comfort.

"Oh my God, how totally disgusting was that guy?" asked Piper.

They were walking down Fifth Avenue, along Central Park. They had decided (or, rather, Piper had decided for them) that they were going to go a few blocks south to Piper's apartment, which was where they always seemed to congregate when they needed to chill, in a low-key way. There were more exciting streets in New York to walk down at this time of night, but the consensus seemed to be that, after the problem in the bar, they should walk down a quiet street so as not to get too overstimulated.

"I've never met anyone more disgusting than that guy," Zach said. "I swear to God, I wanted to *obliterate* him."

Zach was lugging his duffel bag, and it was so sweet to think about him packing so lightly for Paris! Courtney liked that he was so practical.

Zach really was such an amazing guy, such an admirable, stand-up person. The way he'd rushed to Amelia's defense, the way he took care of his twin sister, made Courtney feel as if she were flying. The notion that he would do anything for Amelia nearly took Courtney's breath away. Zach's bravery and his strength were very close to making her fall wildly, completely in love with him. (As if she weren't already.)

And to *think* how tired he must have been after his flight. But Zach was so much more resilient, and so much stronger (mentally stronger, not only physically stronger) than Courtney was. Courtney was always a wreck whenever they flew to or from Europe.

"You two were awesome in there," Geoff said. "Seriously."

You know who *hadn't* been awesome tonight? The only member of their cabal who hadn't proven himself up to the task at hand: Geoff.

This night had clarified so many things for Courtney, including her feelings for Geoff. She regarded him, in his creased khakis and his beautifully pressed Thomas Pink shirt, and she felt nothing. Then she looked at Zach, in his tattered bad-boy shorts and Chuck Taylors.

"Can I ask you guys a question?" Geoff asked.

"Ask away," Piper said. As they were walking and

talking, Piper was simultaneously texting someone (but who?) on her phone. The sky was dark, and the backlight from the phone shone up her face in a kind of eerie way.

"Was *I* okay in there?" Geoff asked.

All four of them stopped in their tracks and stared at Geoff. Surely he didn't *really* want to know, did he? A couple of hours ago Courtney had still found his insecurity endearing, but now it made her uncomfortable. She didn't know how to answer his question.

Fortunately, she didn't have to.

"*Geoff*," Piper replied, "you were *incredible* in the bar. We all were. . . . Hey, did you see that dude's face when I told him my mother always said he was trailer trash or whatever?" asked Piper. "That was hilarious."

Courtney wasn't sure that *hilarious* was the right word. Insulting the guy and his sister had actually made Courtney feel bad, but it had done the trick and made the guy and the girl scamper off like infuriated bunnies.

"You really *do* know everyone," Courtney said. "Where do you know him from?"

Piper laughed. "Oh, I don't. He's probably wondering who the hell my mother is!"

"I don't know," Amelia said. "I think I'm beginning to feel just a little bit sorry for him. Aren't you? I mean, whoever Ann is, sounds like she really did a number on him."

"Oh, Amelia," Zach said. "Always thinking of others, aren't you?"

It was almost as if Zach were saying this as an insult, his tone was so sharp, but Courtney assumed it was just concern in his voice. Courtney had noticed this about Amelia too—that she always tried to understand where everyone was coming from. To be completely accurate, though, Courtney wouldn't say that Amelia was always trying to see the best in everyone; it was more complicated than that. She was trying to figure everyone out.

"I don't know about that, Zach," Amelia said. "But I try."

Zach patted his sister on the back. "Something you learned from Mom, I'm sure."

Amelia and Zach exchanged glances, glances whose deep meaning was understood only to them.

That was the final piece of evidence Courtney needed, wasn't it, that proved that their mother was no longer in their lives?

Suddenly Courtney felt very lucky to have such stellar parents herself. Sure, her father wasn't around as much as she wanted him to be, and yes, she felt that her mother could frequently be pretentious and social-climby, but, really, who cared? Weren't there worse crimes against humanity? Courtney's parents were essentially good people, and they loved her, and probably most important, they were *there*. Amelia and Zach's parents didn't seem to be anywhere. Courtney had never even met their father, who had been with them when they were in St. Bart's, of course, although he was mysteriously absent the whole time.

A thought came to Courtney, something that had never occurred to her before: Amelia and Zach seemed almost like orphans. Wealthy orphans, to be sure, but orphans just the same. There was something so heart-breaking about them—it was as if they'd had to figure out everything for themselves. With Courtney, Piper, and Geoff, life had been a little easier-going: they'd always had everything figured out *for* them.

"My mother taught me a lot too," Piper said. "She taught me how to live on ten calories a day. She taught me that chewing sugar-free gum burns more calories than chewing nothing at all."

"Oh, don't be so bitter, Piper," Geoff said. "She's not *that* bad."

That was just like Piper, Courtney thought, to turn the tone of the conversation negative. Sometimes Courtney loved Piper, and sometimes she just wanted to ignore her. Tonight Courtney wanted to ignore Piper, please. And Geoff.

The trees in Central Park smelled sweet, and the warm summer air felt heavenly on Courtney's face. She, Zach, and Amelia were walking three abreast on the sidewalk, and Piper and Geoff were walking in front of them, side by side. Courtney knew that it had been a challenging night for Amelia (was she still upset, poor thing?), but Courtney was getting in a really good mood. She inched in just a little bit closer to Zach. Could he feel her breathing?

"Are you going to call your father soon?" Courtney asked.

She was curious about the nature of Zach's relationship with his father, but, of a more immediate concern, she wondered when he was going to have to go to Connecticut to look at property for him. She was sort of hoping that he wouldn't have to go to Connecticut until Sunday, because it would be so nice to get to spend the whole day with him—and with Amelia—tomorrow.

"My *father*?" Zach asked.

He shot Amelia a look, as if waiting for her to tell him what to do. How cute was that—and how enlightened for a guy—to look up to his sister the way he did? He really relied on her for help and advice. Courtney's father, who was always full of life advice, had once told her that she should only date men who liked and respected women. That was definitely Zach.

"Zach, you need to call Daddy when we get to Piper's and ask him what the schedule is for tomorrow," Amelia said.

Courtney felt slightly disappointed about tomorrow. But then she had an idea: maybe she could go to Connecticut with him?

"Oh, riiiiight," Zach said. "I need to call Dad. I almost forgot."

Amelia chucked him on the arm. "Zach, you have the *worst* memory. Daddy needs you to look at some property in Connecticut with a Realtor, *remember*?"

Piper turned. She asked, "*Where* in Connecticut?"

"Westport," Amelia said.

"Greenwich," Zach said.

Now Geoff turned. "Well, which is it?"

"*Zach!*" Amelia exclaimed with comic mock exasperation. "You *know* Daddy's interested only in Westport." Then to the group, Amelia said, "Ever since he was a little boy, Zach has been a *wreck* with jet lag. Do you remember, Zach, the time we went to Dubai to see the Sultan of Brunei, and you couldn't even remember what your name was for *days*?"

The Sultan of Brunei. Holy shit. Zach and Amelia had so many fascinating stories to tell, and Courtney was getting greedy to know them all. She wanted to know who Zach and Amelia *were*; she wanted to *understand* them. But would they let her? Would they let her get that deep?

"We should all go to Connecticut tomorrow," Piper said without turning around. "We can make a road trip out of it. My great-auntie lives in Westport, right next to Paul Newman. I think she'll still be in Provence, so we could just stop by there and raid her bar. All top-shelf stuff. Has anyone here ever tried absinthe?"

Geoff sheepishly raised his hand.

Amelia and Zach ignored Piper's question about absinthe.

"I'm not sure everyone jumping in a car and going to Connecticut together sounds like such a good idea," Amelia said. "Our father is a private man, and he likes to keep his real estate transactions, you know . . . *private.*"

Something about that word—*private*—made Courtney's heart turn cartwheels. That was exactly the right word to use to describe Zach and Amelia too. There was a part of each of them that was closed off to Courtney. People with hidden sides were just so much more interesting and alluring. Piper, who was more into the "blurt it out" school, could take some lessons in how to be private.

"What*ever*," Piper said. "Suit yourself. I didn't think you were going to actually *buy* something in Connecticut, but I guess you're planning on moving fast."

Oh, shut up, Piper. Courtney stole a glace at Zach. He was leaning toward Courtney, either from the weight of his small duffel bag, or maybe because he wanted to nudge a little bit closer to her.

Wanting to say something—anything—to Zach,

Courtney asked, "Can I carry your bag for you?"

Zach looked at her and smiled sweetly.

"I don't think so," he said. "But thanks."

"Courtney, you never offered to carry *my* bag before," said Geoff as he linked arms with Piper.

Zach and Courtney exchanged glances, each of them blushing a little.

As they strolled into the gorgeous marble lobby of Piper's building (huge Asian vases with voluptuous peonies in them everywhere, and everything smelled of fresh peonies and old money), Zach shifted his duffel bag to his other arm, to the arm facing his sister. His left arm was now free, and he could do whatever he wanted with it.

That was when he grabbed Courtney's hand.

19

You Can't Change the Past, but You Can Lie About It

FRIDAY NIGHT/SATURDAY MORNING, NEW YORK

In the middle of the night Amelia woke up in a canopied bed. The shades to the bed were drawn, just as if she were a character in a Charles Dickens novel. It took her a few seconds to orient herself. Reality came back, groggily. Amelia was in a guest room in Piper's apartment. They had stayed up drinking until three thirty, and then an executive decision was made by Courtney, dear, sweet, naive Courtney, the only sober one in the bunch, that they should just crash here.

Oh, God, Amelia was so dizzy, and her head hurt, and the inside of her mouth felt like sandpaper—overall, she felt as if she'd been run over by a truck. Usually she knew how to pace her drinking, but last night, not so much. This was the first hangover of her life. If she were feeling more like herself, she'd have been determined to make it her last.

As it was, she invested all her energy into pulling back the thick brocade bed curtain—was it red or purple? she couldn't tell in the dark—and turning on the light by the bed. (Oh, God, that little lamp was bright. BTW, the curtains were purple.) She padded across the beautiful parquetry floor on her way to the door. She needed some water. She really, seriously needed some water. She also wanted to go find Zach, although she had no idea what room he was in.

Amelia wanted to check on Zach, of course, and make sure he hadn't passed out alongside some pristine ten-thousand-dollar Italian toilet somewhere in the vast Hansen apartment, but she also wanted to have a little chat with him. While he certainly hadn't been on his best behavior that night with his little digs at her, she was currently more concerned with what she might've said.

This was the main reason Amelia didn't like to get superdrunk, especially not with people whom she was trying to get on her good side. It was about a hundred times more difficult to keep your stories straight when you were drunk. She had a vague, horrible memory from last night: she couldn't remember who she was supposed to be, what role she was supposed to inhabit. Was she supposed to be an Olympic skier, or a stage actress playing Maria in the upcoming Broadway revival of *West Side Story*, or a budding philanthropist from a fabulously wealthy Main Line family? These had all been useful lies in the past, lies that had gotten her whatever she had temporarily needed, but Amelia was trying to keep the past behind her now. She would totally erase the past if she could.

It wasn't as though the past had ever gotten her anywhere.

Finally, after so many years of confusion and struggle, she had found the world she belonged to. She hoped, though, that that world wanted her as much as she wanted it.

Last night, when they'd walked into the grand entranceway of Piper's apartment (which Amelia had seen pictures of in both *Elle Decor* and *Architectural Digest*), Amelia considered not only the swirling staircase and the chandeliers, but she also considered her wonderful new friends, Courtney, Piper, and Geoff. Everything in her new life was finally perfect, so, so perfect. Exactly as it always should've been.

Later, when they were ensconced in Piper's father's gleaming wood-paneled library, getting wasted on his Scotch (brought back from a recent vacation in the Scottish Highlands), Amelia began to feel all paranoid and insecure. Was Amelia—were her *lies—good enough* for them?

The last thing she remembered: Piper gossiping about some girl who had passed her that day on that stupid socialite-ranking website, saying that she was only twenty, but that she'd already had collagen injections, Botox, and breast implants.

"It was so lame," Piper said. "For, like, a month after she got her boobs done, she couldn't bend over or reach up. When I was at her house on Fire Island, she kept making me bend over to clean up her dog's poop."

Amelia had been feeling really drunk already, although they would stay up for two more hours. She had a question that she couldn't shake: how much did breast implants cost? If she hadn't been as drunk, she wouldn't have asked it. Not that *she* was thinking about getting breast implants, or anything . . .

"How much does it cost?" Amelia asked.

Piper, Geoff, and Zach had looked at her as if she had lice. Courtney, good old nice Courtney, was the only one who didn't flash her a look of bewilderment/contempt. Truly wealthy people didn't have to ask how much things cost.

"How much does *what* cost?" Piper asked.

Amelia didn't see a way out of this one.

"A . . . breast implant," Amelia said, feeling like a total idiot. Her heart skipped several beats; she had revealed herself as a sad coupon clipper, as someone who only bought things on sale, as someone who was always looking for a bargain. She had outed herself as a *poor person*.

Oh, God, they could tell she was poor.

Geoff was on the other side of the room, lying on one of the many couches. He got up and refilled his rocks glass from the crystal decanter.

"Does anyone in this room really know how much *anything* costs?" he asked.

And then, all at once, everyone started cracking up. Amelia and Zach caught each other's eyes, because of course they knew the prices of *everything*. (Amelia always believed that she would have made a very good contestant on *The Price Is Right*.) But right then, in that room that was bigger than their entire apartment in New Hampshire, lounging on luxurious fabric that would take their hypereducated father (who was so much more educated than anyone else's parents, even—especially—those with more money) years to save up to buy, none of that mattered.

Amelia helped herself to another glass of Scotch, and then another one. That was sort of when the rest of the night became one big blur. And now, as Amelia groped for the doorknob in one of Piper's guest rooms, she felt terrified that she'd said something else that might have revealed her for who she was.

Amelia needed to find Zach so he could reassure her. First, though, she needed that glass of water.

Was Piper's apartment actually bigger than Courtney's? The long hallway down which Amelia walked was illuminated by wall sconces; it seemed as if there were about twenty closed doors, each probably leading into another dream room. Which room was Zach's? Which room was Piper's? Geoff's? Courtney's?

It was too crazy to think that Zach and Courtney had somehow ended up in the same room, right? They had been secretly holding hands when they walked into Piper's place, and in Piper's dad's library they had sat on opposite ends of the same couch . . . when everyone else—Amelia, Piper, and Geoff—had all been lounging on their own private couches or upholstered benches.

But Amelia hadn't seen any sparks between them on the couch—Courtney was too prim and proper, and sitting with perfect posture, her hands delicately placed in her lap as if she were waiting to be asked to dance at a debutante ball. And Zach seemed to get more and more morose and quieter and quieter as the night wore on, and totally missed his opportunity to make a move on Courtney.

Amelia knew that Zach was mad at her. She could guess why, although his anger was, she believed, unfair.

She counted the reasons why he was pissed at her: she'd lied that he'd been in Paris, she'd lied that he worked for the president of France, she'd lied that he could speak French, and she'd lied that he had to go to Connecticut tomorrow to look at property for their father. And *he'd* had to lie about the dude in the bar, and tell Courtney, Piper, and Geoff that Sam had mistaken her for someone else. He was probably also mad that he had to break up another fight between Amelia and some ex-boyfriend. It was a sad fact of life that these kinds of situations seemed to come up a lot.

The bigger, overarching reason Zach was probably mad at her: whatever lies Amelia came up with immediately became his lies too. He had no choice but to follow her.

But shouldn't he be grateful? Look where Amelia's lies had gotten him.

Amelia took a turn down another long, illuminated hallway. There were lots of closed doors in this hallway too. Lining the walls, between each of the rooms, were French Empire chests of drawers with ornate gold handles. Amelia thought about pulling open one of those drawers to see what was inside. (Would there be stacks of money? Gold coins? Vials filled with the blood of virgins?) But she decided against snooping. Piper was her friend now, and she didn't want to violate their tender new bond.

She turned another corner and realized she was totally lost. She looked behind her, then to her left, then to her right. Every single view looked exactly the same.

Amelia had no idea where she had come from, or where she was going, and she suddenly felt overcome by terror.

"*Ann*," came a deep voice from one of the many hallways.

Amelia spun around.

In back of her, sitting on one of the chests of drawers, was Piper, her face illuminated by the glow of her iPhone.

"What are you doing up, *Ann*?" Piper asked.

Her voice sounded really weird, as if it had dropped at least two octaves.

Now, suddenly, Amelia couldn't remember why she was awake and wandering the hallway. Was she looking for the bathroom? Was she snooping? Was she looking for Geoff's room, and did she want to sleep with him?

Oh, and why was Piper so creepily calling her Ann? Amelia didn't like that, not at all.

"I was just looking for the bathroom," Amelia said.

Amelia took a step toward Piper. She was wearing shorts and a Hawthorne T-shirt, although Piper Hansen went to Choate, not to Hawthorne, as everyone who was anyone knew.

"Why do you keep calling me Ann?" she asked.

"Because I like calling people by their real name."

Amelia was sweating. She looked down. She was still wearing the dress from tonight, the one Courtney had loaned her. She was a wrinkled, disheveled mess. Suddenly she was very aware that she was wearing someone else's clothes. And why was she wearing someone else's clothes? Because she couldn't afford her own.

"Why do you think my name is Ann?" Amelia asked.

She attempted a light, lilting, laughing tone. She expected—she *hoped*—the answer would be that Piper had heard the drunk dude at the bar call her Ann.

"Because I know everything there is to know about you," Piper said.

Amelia suddenly didn't feel drunk, or hungover, or sleepy, or headachy in the least. What she felt was acutely, quiveringly alert, as if she had infrared vision, as if she could see distant planets and the mountains and craters on them.

Amelia, because she was feeling very bold, and also because she felt as if she had nothing to lose, had another question to ask: "And what else do you know about me?"

Piper hopped down off the chest and walked over to the light switch. She flicked her hand upward, and the lights on the walls were illuminated to their full wattage.

It was as if Amelia were being interrogated by the police. She blinked from the pain of the harsh lights, but Piper had no reaction, as if the light didn't bother her at all.

"Let's seeeeee," Piper said. "I know the most important thing about you."

Amelia felt sick. She felt like running away or sinking into the parquetry floor. She knew that Amelia's father was a marginally employed traveling classics lecturer, one who seemed uniquely unqualified to even be considered for tenure anywhere? She knew that Amelia's mother had never felt one speck of love for either of her two children—never felt one speck of love for anyone other than *herself*—and had run away from her godforsaken family at the earliest possible chance, leaving them heartbroken and in tatters?

"*What?*" Amelia asked.

"Wellllll," Piper said.

This was going to be bad. This was going to be very, very bad and terrible. Amelia could feel it in her bones.

"I know that you dated that dude in the bar from tonight."

That was Piper's big reveal? That Amelia had dated Sam?! Who cared? No one cared! No one cared anything about *that* idiot guy. Dating him was one of the least important and most innocuous and forgettable things Amelia had ever done. In fact, she should have gotten a medal or some kind of award for dating him.

"I *did* date him!" Amelia exclaimed. She could never have imagined she would someday be *proud* to admit that she had dated that moron. "Guilty as charged!"

Immediately Amelia realized her mistake: by admitting she'd dated Sam, she'd just owned up to lying.

"So then *he* wasn't the guilty one tonight," Piper said. "He was telling the truth."

Amelia and Piper stared at each other for what felt like forever, while Amelia considered her next move. She caught a glimpse of an antique sword displayed on the wall and wished not for the first time in her young life that she'd been born in another time, when people settled their issues with duels.

Offing your enemy was definitely one way to solve a problem.

"Yes," Amelia said at last. "He was telling the truth about that part."

"Well, then, we have to talk about your taste in men," Piper said.

Piper's face hardened for a split second before she let out something between a laugh and a sigh.

"Oh, don't worry; I've seen the light." Amelia felt as if there were a conversation going on beneath their conversation, but she wasn't exactly sure what it was.

"I'm sure you have." Piper yawned and then dropped

her iPhone into her shorts pocket.

"I'm going back to bed," she said. "But I just found out I have an extra ticket to the New York Philharmonic for tomorrow night. Do you want to go with me?"

Amelia wasn't sure if the moment had truly passed or if this was part of Piper's game. But one thing she knew about Piper was that she didn't suffer fools. The invitation was genuine, for sure. It was the motive that concerned Amelia.

"Are you kidding?" Amelia asked. "My aunt is a world-famous cellist. I *love* the symphony," she said, lying again.

Lying, as always.

Piper paused for several beats longer than was comfortable.

"Great," she said finally. "See you in the morning." And then Piper leaned in for a cheek kiss, a small gesture that spoke volumes in its sincerity.

Hello, beautiful world, thought Amelia Warner as she drew Piper Hansen into the most heartfelt hug the world had ever known.

Want to find out if Amelia
claims her place in the Beautiful World?

Look for

EVERYTHING AND MORE

the next book in the series.

Welcome to Wellington: Just because you're rich, brilliant, and perfect in every way doesn't mean you can survive boarding school.

Check out the first three novels in the Upper Class series!

The Upper Class

No one ever thinks they'll crash and burn in their first semester—but someone always does.

Laine is a born Wellington girl: rich, sophisticated, blond. Nikki is everything a Wellington girl shouldn't be: outlandish, sexy, from a new money family. Laine and Nikki couldn't have less in common. But to survive first semester, they may have to stick together—or risk being the first girl to go down in flames.

Miss Educated

Just because you survived first semester doesn't mean you can relax.

Chase is this close to being expelled from the prestigious Wellington Academy. Parker, on the other hand, is doing just fine academically—it's her social life that's on probation. When a campus tragedy and a little fate bring Chase and Parker together, Wellington finally starts to make sense to them both. If only it wasn't so easy to mess everything up.

Off Campus

A new year at Wellington means new students, new drama, and the same old rule: Don't get caught.

Nikki is an old pro at the boarding school thing now. She's ready to show someone else the ropes, someone like Delia. A transfer student with a dark past, Delia doesn't quite fit in anywhere, but she sure knows how to have fun. But when fun leads to sneaking off campus, it can very quickly turn dangerous.

www.harperteen.com

What does it take to be part of the In Crowd in the most "in" zip code in the country—

Becky Miller is about to find out!

Sixteen-year-old Becky Miller goes to school with the glamorous children of Hollywood's elite—and has never really fit in. But with her best friend moving away, her parents getting divorced, and her therapist gone AWOL, now might be the perfect time to try. What's she got to lose?